The
Phone

and Other Short Stories

Gary Paul Bryant

Deliberate Content

DEDICATION

This little book is dedicated to Gleason Snickell

CONTENTS

ACKNOWLEDGMENTS

I would thank Mr. Ford in 4th grade English who showed me how boring and unpleasant the written word could be without breaking a few rules. I want to thank my brother Bill, for introducing me to Mark Twain, John Steinbeck and Jules Verne, and to everyone who has offered their feedback and editing skills over the years, including Ben, Vicki, Jerry, Arlene and of course, Roger. Most of all, I want to thank you, dear reader, for your continued support of independent authors, no matter how the words find their way to you.

Cover design by DeliberateContent.com

THE PHONE

Cyryl Smith lived alone above a beauty parlor on Bank St. in New London, Connecticut. His wife had died of ovarian cancer at the insufficient age of thirty-six. Now, with his own diabetes, arthritis, intermittent shingles and dementia, Cyryl Smith spent much of his time ruminating about his past. At sixty-eight, he felt that he was too young to die, but didn't really relish the idea of living in such an annoying state of health. He deflected these thoughts the best he could with imagined trips into his childhood years while scouring the Internet for names of his grade school friends, looking for hints into the outcomes of their own lives.

He wasn't sure how he really felt whenever he came across a classmate's obituary. "I win!" He would say out loud upon the discovery that Tom Rakuza was a recent fatality in an auto accident. Life had simply become a game of survival. The purpose of living, he decided, was simply about out-living everybody else, no matter how miserable his own life became. This was a simpler explanation then the real one; he was simply lonely.

At Nathan Hale Elementary in the late nineteen fifties, Cyryl spent most of his time reading. He had a good memory, and schoolwork came easily, but that didn't mean he would excel. Cyryl Smith made a conscious decision to 'just get by.' Cyryl saw for himself two choices: He could use his bonus time and energy to 'excel' at school work and be more than adequate, or he could explore the world, starting with girls. He chose the latter.

As much as he might have liked to, Cyryl had a difficult time making friends. He had only two that he could count on during his formative years, Andrew Ment and Rowena Dombrowski. Everyone had stupid names back then. His own real name was Cyryl Karastanovitski; he was a Polish Jew, born on a boat, under a tarp, smuggled out from behind the Iron Curtain, in pouring April rain in 1953. He never met his mother. The story was that she apparently died giving birth, but Cyryl was not convinced of its authenticity. Today Cyryl Smith walks the streets of New London Connecticut, most sunny spring days, poking into antique shops, feeding the three pigeons that reside in dormers of the old fire station on Bank St. He still keeps in touch with Andrew Ment who is the only other childhood classmate that remained in New London. They'd occasionally meet at Dunkin Donuts for coffee and argue about the Yankees and Red Sox. Neither man was a baseball fan. In fact, Cyryl had never been to a single baseball game in his entire life, while Andrew had lost his father to a heart attack at Fenway Park when Andrew was just fifteen years old.

For nearly forty years Cyryl had lead a simple life. After two tours of duty in Vietnam in 1974, he returned to New London to marry his childhood sweetheart Rowena, only to lose her six years later. He went through a series of minimum wage jobs until he found a position at Amalgamated Grocery as an expediter, where he stayed until he retired.

On this day, Cyryl said goodbye to Andrew after their usual morning coffee, but this time decided to proceed down Shaw Street. His plan was to head up Willet Avenue and walk back on Ocean Avenue. On Shaw Street he noticed a new antique store. He went inside. The place was stocked from top to bottom, from the back to the front with thousands of contrivances, garments and garaged sale'd items of long ago. He couldn't see anyone in the place but he could hear an old woman talking loudly, apparently on the phone, in a back room, her shrill voice echoing through the seemingly endless aisles of aging junk. Cyryl spied an old incandescent light bulb shining brightly through a hole in the back wall, a hole the size of a Maxwell House coffee can. Cigarette smoke rhythmically bellowed through the hole like some kind of special effect you'd see at a carnival amusement, the voice alternating with the smoke.

Cyryl looked around the room. The floor to the right was covered in old suitcases and satchels; satchels of the type once used by rural doctors of the last century; suitcases and sea trunks too large for any one man to carry; old musty cases filled with tired old air and retired memories.

On a table to his left he focused on his own brand of ancient eye candy. Electronics – electrics really, from the mid-twentieth century, they hadn't quite figured out the 'tronic' part yet. He wasn't surprised to see the cluster of old table top radios, the basket of ancient 'tubes', those multi-pronged glass canisters that somehow were the magic pellets of radio prior to 1970. He recognized all of it. His own father had been a TV and radio hobbyist in the forties and fifties, spending most of his weekends hunkered down in the basement rummaging through a hoard of cryptic capacitors, ruminating resistors and cathartic condensers. These items, in combination with the previously mentioned tubes, were then stuffed into old wooden cases to become radios, worthy of Jack Benny and the Lone Ranger.

What he didn't expect to see was the phone. Sitting atop a peach basket chock full of old telephones and medieval answering machines, was "his phone," his mom's rotary phone. The family number was still visible in the center of the dialer. It was the phone that was picked up at 3:15 AM when Uncle Mort told his dad that his mother had died of kidney failure in 1957. It was the phone that rang when his sister called home from her first Thanksgiving away at college in 1962. It was the phone Cyryl used to call Rowena Dombrowski, almost every night starting in 7th grade under the premise of getting homework assignments. It was the phone he used on March 13, 1969 to ask Rowena to the prom. He pulled it out of the basket, interrupted the still talking-on-the-phone clerk by intentionally banging the lower counter with his foot. Feigning embarrassed surprise, as if he had made the noise by accident, he presented his phone to the still smoke-spewing clerk along with the full seven dollar asking price, and then took it home.

He stared at the dated contraption for several minutes before plugging it into the phone jack. He picked up the receiver and what he heard startled him. It was the dial tone. He slammed the receiver down. Suddenly more memories came flooding back. How he longed for those days.

Rowena was knitting a sweater for her mother's birthday when the phone rang. It was probably Cyryl, she said to herself. It was his habit to call her almost every day to get homework assignments. Rowena wasn't stupid, however, and she knew this was just a pretense to talk to her. "Whatcha doing?" he would say more than a few times. Each time he called, the conversation would last longer and longer. She tried not to admit she liked him, but she always looked forward to his calls.

This call was for her mother. Apparently, the Bouchattis down the street were getting a color TV. No one she knew had ever seen one before. Rowena began to wonder why Cyryl hadn't called her yet.

Above the beauty parlor in the humid and hot afternoon, Cyryl ignored his growling stomach and picked up the receiver again. He wondered who had the family phone number now. He dialed. It rang once, and again, after seven rings he hung up.

Cyryl picked up the phone again and dialed a different number. On the third ring someone picked up. "Hello?" the young voice answered.

Cyryl was taken aback, he recognized the voice. He also recognized the impossibility of that voice. It was Rowena Dombrowski. Her faint Polish accent would betray her anywhere. Yet it was in fact, impossible.

They had gone to their high school prom together, escorted by her older brother, who drove the family car. Neither of them knew how to dance. It wasn't long before they had escaped the prom and simply spent the next two hours walking through the city's quiet neighborhoods holding hands, not speaking.

She had gone on to college, he had not. When Jeff was born life changed for both of them. She relished her new role as a mother, while he took on a second job to help pay the expenses. They never had a vacation, but somehow found happiness on the weekends and in their new found purpose; their family. When his wife died, Cyryl

4

was devastated. He was also embarrassed that his son was able to cope with her loss better than he, or so it seemed. They never spoke about it much. They both knew that without Rowena, there wasn't much to hold them together. They eventually drifted apart despite playing their respective familial roles almost perfectly.

"Hello," he replied, "who am I speaking with?"

"This is Rowena, sir."

Cyryl began to sweat. His heart was beating fast now. "Can… May I speak with you father?"

"My father passed away sir, a long time ago."

"I'm sorry to hear that." Cyryl said as he frantically searched for words. "I… I knew him as a child."

"Oh!" Rowena replied, "and to whom am I speaking?" using a phrase she had recently heard on television.

Cyryl Smith slammed down the phone. This was all too insane. It wasn't possible, he thought to himself.

Cyryl was pacing around the room, stopped suddenly and went back to the phone. He dialed another number.

"Hello?" said the man on the other end.

"Hello, could I speak with Andrew, please?" Cyryl replied.

"He's not here right now; I think he's playing baseball or something with his friends. He should be home by suppertime" Mr. Ment answered.

"Right" Cyryl said, "I'll try later." He hung up. His phone was calling his childhood.

Rowena had not told her mother about the strange phone call she received yesterday. She didn't understand why the man had hung up on her so abruptly. He had said that he had known her father when they were young. Rowena didn't know anything at all about her father, except that he was Polish and had escaped from the Nazis during the War.

Rowena wondered why Cyryl had not called her. But this pause in his pursuit of her gave her time to decide that she really did like him. They would probably end up in high school together, she thought, unless he goes to the private school over by the Coast Guard Academy, but she didn't think he would. She wondered if they would ever date "for real."

Just then the phone rang. Cyryl! She thought as she ran to the phone.

"Hello?" she sputtered, out of breath.

"Oh, hello Rowena, I'm the friend of your father; I had to call to apologize for hanging up so suddenly the other day. I..."

Rowena was at first disappointed that it wasn't Cyryl, but now she was intrigued. This man had called again. She thought it might be her chance to learn something about her father.

"Think nothing of it," she said. "You probably had to go to the bathroom or something."

"Yes, that's it, I had to go to the bathroom, I'm very sorry."

"You said you knew my father, can you tell me about him?"

Cyryl hadn't planned on calling her back. He didn't want to. He knew he came off as foolish when he hung up and wasn't sure if he was sane any longer, whether or not this was all a strange dream, or nightmare.

On the other end of the line was a young girl, who in about four years' time would become his wife, eight years before she would make him a widower.

Cyryl struggled for something to say, he had no idea who her father was and he had, of course, never met him. He searched his memory for any hints she may have given him.

"Your father? Well, he was Polish of course, from Poland actually - before the Nazis invaded."

"You said you knew him when you were young. Do you mean in Poland?" Rowena had heard this voice before, but she wasn't sure where.

"Yes, in Poland, we both worked in a bottle factory for a time, he was a foreman. He was the boss."

"Was he your boss?" Rowena asked.

"You bet, my boss, everybody's boss." Cyryl was clearly uncomfortable now. He had crossed a line. He began to think of the repercussions of this cross-time conversation. Was he building false hopes? Telling her lies?

"I'm sorry Rowena, but I must hang up now. It has been nice speaking with you."

"You're hanging up already? But you haven't really told me about my father!"

"I'll call you again soon, I promise," Cyryl replied. He hung up the phone.

Looking around the room he had lived in the last 25 years he couldn't find a single memory he wanted to keep. The room was empty in more ways the one. He missed Rowena.

Rowena's mom came home just as she put down the phone.

"Look honey, Swanson TV dinners tonight!" Rowena's mom loved American technology; toasters, television, Polaroid cameras and now TV dinners. She was as proud of this new American ingenuity as if she had invented it herself.

Rowena had tasted TV dinners before. It was supposed to be a big treat. She didn't get it. Turkey, roast beef or American Chop Suey – which was really macaroni in a tomato sauce- all tasted like cat poop to Rowena.

"Cat poop" she said half-out loud.

"What was that dear?" her mom askedS.

"Nothing Mom, TV dinners sound great."

Just then the phone rang again. This time it was Cyryl.

"Watcha doing?" he asked.

"Cyryl! Where have you been, you haven't called me for days!" She was surprised at herself for revealing so much of her emotion to him. Cyryl didn't seem to notice.

"I'm having trouble with geography," he said.

"Really?" asked Rowena.

"No, not really. I just wanted to talk to you."

Rowena smiled to herself.

In the apartment above the beauty parlor, Cyryl could feel the late afternoon heat beat on him through the window. He wanted to pull the shade and close the curtains. There was no shade. There were no curtains. There was a knock on the door.

"Dad, are you in there, Dad?"

Cyryl heard keys rattle and then the door opened.

"I've been looking all over for you! We've all been worried sick, I've been worried!"

"Sorry," was all Cyryl could mutter.

Jeff Smith, Cyryl's only son, found his father sitting on the floor of an empty apartment, staring at the only other object in the room, an old fashioned telephone.

"Where'd that phone come from, Dad? I thought we got all of your stuff out of here last month?"

"I bought it at that new antique shop on Shaw. It's my old family phone, Jeff," Cyryl replied proudly.

"Ok, you can take it with you, but we've got to get going. Dinner is waiting."

Jeff helped Cyryl from the floor, handing him his phone. "Got it?" Jeff asked.

"Yes," came the one word reply. He loved his son, but they just never connected. Jeff never had time to talk, always awkward on the phone. That was one thing about Rowena though; she always liked getting his phone calls.

A MAN OF PROVERBS

When Bobby Adedge was 18 years old, he had already won two Olympic gold medals. By the time he was twenty-two, he had been a well-known goalie on a professional hockey team. He had married an even more famous supermodel, who had her own budding career as an actress. He thought himself to be smart, having invented the first dissolvable hockey puck, which was great for planet Earth and recycling, but not-so-good when hockey games went into overtime, the puck often melting onto the ice before the game was over. His inventor-phase was short-lived.

Now, all of that is gone. His wife began an affair with Lionel-the-clichéd-pool-boy, and eventually started a new chlorinated bacteria-free life with him. She believed, having been convinced that if she paid for Lionel's college education, that he was certain to be a successful manufacturer of probiotics, selling them directly to disenchanted national healthcare participants.

Bobby Adedge had been an optimistic man. He spent much of his hockey fortune traveling the world, experiencing other cultures, their art and music. There was hardly a seventh wonder he hadn't visited at least seven times. Over time, he developed into a well-educated old-fashioned liberal, not in the political sense, but in the classical sense of worldly appreciation.

By his mid-thirties he had pretty much run out of ways to entertain himself. He also ran out of money. He started looking for new ways to support his pastime, which he could not precisely identify.

He finally settled on becoming a greeting card writer. His mother had remarked that Bobby had never been at a loss for words. His father concurred. "He would never shut up," Bob Sr. always said.

It was true enough that Bobby's always found an artful way of putting an experience into unforgettable prose; he had an unusual gift of writing proverbs.

"To be or not to be." That wasn't a question to Bobby Adedge, it was an ultimatum.

He was trying to decide if this little word play conundrum would be suitable for a greeting card. It was not. Still, he changed the font to **Impact** and resized the text to 60 points, centered it and clicked print.

He posted it on the wall with masking tape. It was the second thing the paramedics saw when they found the body.

"Just because you discover that you've dug yourself a hole, doesn't mean you have to keep digging to China," he would say out loud to his empty living room, squint, then type it out.

"Just because you've fallen into a well doesn't mean you have to swim to the bottom," was another variation on his optimistic view of inevitable hopelessness.

Yes, he thought himself better at coining maxims, tweaking a motto here and there, giving a sharp edge to an old saw. His work was the epitome of the epigram, it inspired, energized, enlivened the fabric of the world he was part of. He discovered that his words had power over others, but now these words were coming to have an even stronger power over himself.

Bobby Adedge had a good life, at least for nine years, six months and 23 days of it. It started when he made the varsity hockey team in

Saskatoon. but that richly fulfilling life he loved so much ended in three stages, in three days, over three dinners at three different restaurants in three different cities. He now finds himself simultaneously in three different moods.

Bobby Adedge is a forty-five year old man who sits in his apartment writing proverbs for greeting cards and calendars. He takes his job seriously.

The phone rang. It was his brother Carl. Carl hated sports, but loved his brother, but when Bobby was a hockey star, Carl hated him too. Now that he was a marginal failure like himself, they had something in common, and Carl decided to apply an new affection for his younger brother.

"How's the greeting card business?" Carl asked in earnest.

"It's like a cold day in a hot summer," said Bobby, "It's surprisingly uncalled for," Bobby announced paternalistically, having ad-libbed that one right off the top of his head. He squinted once, and wrote it down.

"Listen," Carl continued," I've got two tickets to the Bruins for tonight, how about it?"

Bobby squinted, "The ball's in your court, Carl, mine are resting comfortably right here with me for the remains of the day, not unlike the movie."

"Ok Bobby, I'll talk to you tomorrow." Carl hung up the phone, not having a clue as what his brother was babbling about.

Bobby looked at the clock, "Time marches on," he said to himself, knowing full-well that it was a hackneyed cliché. Bobby did not squint or write it down.

Three weeks went by and Bobby had created more than eighty new greeting card messages. "Cheer Up!, You're only dead twice! Once before the second and the other after the first!" Bobby put this quote in the 'Optimistic' folder. Bobby started thinking about death.

"What if there was an afterlife? Would there be greeting cards for those people just finding that out after the fact?" He mused. He folded a blank piece of paper into a greeting card and scribbled on the front.

"Surprise! " It reads. He opened the card and scribbled the following text on the opposing page.

"…and you thought you were having a birthday tomorrow!"

There was a knock on the door.

"Who is it?" Bobby shouted, barely looking up from his computer screen.

"It's your mother," the voice from behind the door announced.

Bobby started to get up from his chair, hesitated and then sat back down. He used his legs to launch himself and his Office Depot simulated leather $99 roller-wheeled business chair across the Parqay floor. He misjudged the amount of thrust he needed to make the trip and his nose collided with the front door's antique glass doorknob with a considerable commitment.

Blood was streaming out of both nostrils as Bobby struggled to maintain composure and unlock the door. When the elderly Mrs. Adedge first laid eyes on her bloodied son, she nearly fainted. She tried to regain her balance as she grasped for the door knob, which was also dripping with his warm rouge-colored essence. Her fleeting composure allowed her just enough time to consider that the slippery feeling her door-knobbed hand felt was caused by the blood from her son's swollen nose. Her own face went white, and she fell quickly; and would have hit the floor if it had not been for Bobby, still sitting in his chair. On her short trip to the floor, her forehead hit him in the nose one more time for good measure.

After the paramedics took his mother away, having suffered a minor concussion, Bobby and his bandaged nose finally had the quiet time he required to make sense of this unique experience.

"Only a face a mother nose!" He said to himself, in his best nasally Mr. Peabody voice.

"A mother's love nose no bounds!"

"When opportunity knocks, one never nose what might fall in your lap."

"The blood of the son doesn't always fall far from the tree."

For a brief moment, Bobby Adedge thought that the last one might be a stretch, but the moment was indeed brief. He squinted once and wrote it down.

Looking out the window at the ambulance, waving goodbye, he

couldn't help but notice what a production this whole episode had been. He had simply called 911 because his mother fainted over the sight of a little blood. So what did they do? The sent a fire truck and an ambulance and finally a police car! That was a total of nine public employees burning up gallons of fuel in three separate fuel inefficient vehicles to service one fainting old lady.

Bobby wondered if he had subconsciously thwarted his mother's attempt to invite him on a trip to Europe. He didn't want to hurt her feelings by turning her down, but he knew his work was too important to leave behind.

"No time like today for doing tomorrow's work," he said to himself, squinting and writing that nugget down.

A woman going by the Facebook moniker of Mary Gold-Bosom had been sending him notes through his Facebook account. She had collected over two hundred and fifty-six of his greeting cards. Mary had intended to send the first fifteen she had purchased to relatives and friends for their birthdays and anniversaries, but found Bobby's writing style too compelling to part with. She didn't send a single one, and in fact, she collected every card he had ever produced. She was a fan. A fan that wanted to marry him.

At first, Bobby didn't respond to her, but after a while he found that the innocent communication between them inspired him to compose even better card prose for Valentine's Day breakups- which is what he planned to do to Mary Gold-Bosom, as soon as she accepted his marriage proposal. Bobby was not the cold heartless person that his actions might lead one to believe. On the contrary, he was absorbed in his quest to develop the most emotional card copy he could imagine. The fact that he seemed insensitive to the people around him, and the fact he had no real talent for writing, did not stop him. "After all, isn't that how most people made their way through life?"

"When life hands you lemons, try brewing beer." He loved that one.

It was about 10 PM when Bobby finished his last greeting card of the day. He shut off the computer, got up from his chair, and went to the kitchen to get some ice cream. He started to think about the last five years. It had taken Bobby most of that time to figure out what everyone else already knew: that the proverbs he coined encouraged his own isolation. Each and every one of those trite little contrivances was one more vote to retreat from a world he used to embrace.

After all, he had been a hockey professional, yet now he couldn't even attend a sports event with this own brother. He had spent years traveling the world, yet now he couldn't find time to take his own mother to Europe. And as for women, he knew his relationships were shallow, but for them, he had less sympathy. The women he had known in his own life were shallower still.

When Bobby was finished with his ice cream, he put his dish in the sink, rinsed it out with hot water, and laid it on the dish rack to dry. He noticed the freezer door was still open. He turned and, using his left hand, slammed it shut with a sigh.

It was at that moment he felt the stabbing pain in his chest, the stiffness in his jaw, and the sweat beginning to accumulate on his brow. He had seen enough TV to know he was having a heart attack. He knew exactly what to do. He sat down at his desk, took his phone out of his pocket, laid it on the table, grabbed pen and paper, squinted, and began to write a new quotation.

"What kills you, usually does a good job of it the first time around."

"If I knew life was going to be this short, I would have started getting bored earlier."

"That white light you see just before you die, it's not God, it's just a nurse on a cell phone."

Bobby was having trouble breathing now. He reached for his phone, but the pain in his left arm was too great. His right hand still had a pen in it. He wouldn't put it down. Then he said, "OK Google, call 911, speakerphone."

The phone's screen lit up just like the white light you see just before you die. There was a ring. And then: "911. What is your emergency?" said the voice on the smart phone.

"I think I'm having a heart attack." Bobby said, strangely calm now, debating the pros and cons of staying alive, which would mean writing greeting cards for ten or twenty more years.

"Stay calm, sir. What is your address, we'll send you help right away." the voice replied.

"You'll send somebody?" Bobby responded.

"Yes sir, but I need your address. What is your address please sir?"

"Right. You'll be sending a fire truck, and an ambulance and maybe even a police car, is that right?"

The 911 operator was busy working with her GPS triangulation service to determine Bobby's location. Unlike land lines, 911 cell phone location services were still fairly limited. It was going to take a little time.

"Sir, we'll be sending anything you like, but I need to have your address."

"My address, what about yours? Are you wearing a dress? In fact, I think I see a devil with a blue dress. No that was Mitch Ryder and the Detroit Wheels. No, cars are made in Detroit, which might have Michelin tires that may or may not have been manufactured in Wheeling. Nine-one-one person, you are confusing me!"

Bobby tried writing another proverb:

"If I have only one life to give to my country, let me live it as a blonde."

"Sir, Sir! Do you live at the Madison Street Apartments? Sir?"

"That's me!" he said, and those were Bobby's last words.

Such a brilliant life to begin with, a life ultimately whittled down into a hackneyed greeting card writer, trying to find some self-respect by earning a meager living of his own design. So there you have it: An international champion, not only of sports but of generous human experience, ending life on Earth as a simple old Adedge.

THE BITTER CLIMB

When Mark saw Mount Robson come into view, he knew his troubles would soon be over. It was the Canadian Thanksgiving but just another weekend in mid-October for most of the people he knew back in Oakland. The sky was clear and Robson had a new dusting of snow at the seven-thousand foot level. He and his three climbing partners were going to attempt the Kain Face on the north east side of the peak. His sister Caitlin had decided to come on this trip at the last minute. Though they had climbed together in Europe, Caitlin had not always felt close to her brother. It was her idea to try to 'bond' with her brother on this trip.

The helicopter dropped suddenly and descended into Rearguard Meadow on the north side of the mountain. Their gear was dumped quickly and unceremoniously into a single pile. In a few moments the helicopter was gone, leaving the team in silence.

Caitlin could not help but be swept up in the awesome beauty of her new surroundings. "Will the weather hold?" she asked, realizing for the first time just how hard their climb was going to be.

"Everything checks out," Shimm responded. He knew that Caitlin was just trying to get her brother to speak to her, having ridden most of the way from California in total silence. Shimm was not looking forward to this climb ever since he found out Caitlin was a member of the team. His experience so far, was bearing out his anxiety.

Neither Shimm nor Meadows, Mark's closest friends and climbing partners, wanted her to come along.

Meadows saw her as a distraction. "She's too good looking," he would say, "leave her home."

All at once the group began sorting gear, stuffing equipment into backpacks as if the ritual had been rehearsed dozens of times - it had. Crampons, boots, ice axes, gators, water bottles, food, the list was impressive. In about twenty minutes, the big heap of gear was neatly stowed on the backs of the four climbers.

Shimm found Caitlin to be a bore. He fumed as he listened to her nonstop chatter about her years back East at Smith college in Massachusetts.

"We used to practice technical climbing up near Franconia Notch on weekends back at Smith," she would say.

"There are no mountains back East," Meadows would tell her.

"Oh but there are!" she would shoot back, not realizing she had just been bated.

"No, there aren't," agreed Shimm, "the Rockies, those are mountains. The Cascades, again mountains, but back East they just have hills."

"What about Mount Washington?" Caitlin responded, "That's a mountain!"

Mark suddenly stopped his preoccupation with his pack adjustments, looked Caitlin straight in the eyes and said, "Mt. Washington is a wimpy 6,288 feet above sea level. At the summit the wind barely gets to 231 miles per hour, and is generally well-known to be a modest but familiar hill in New Hampshire. It just so happens that there is, in fact, a state bearing the same name that has far more respectful summits."

Everyone laughed. The ice was broken. The team began their trek to the summit of Mount Robson, a real mountain to be sure.

While everyone was enjoying the unusual sunshine, all of them were well aware that Robson was a magnet for bad weather. The route was no picnic, with the final summit push expected to take more than ten hours.

Caitlin was leading the group as they approached the bergschrund. As she leaped across the opening from ice pack to rock, she twisted her foot and lost her footing. She found herself several feet into the chasm, wedged tightly in the cold narrow space.

"Well, we're screwed now," Mark mumbled to no one in particular. He was more concerned with the possibility of abandoning the climb than recovering his sister from the extremely cold cavity she was jammed in.

Meadows was having trouble with his pack straps, "Maybe we should get your sister out of the bergschrund before, you know, she freezes to death? Just a thought," he added.

It took about forty minutes for the three climbers to extract Caitlin from the ice and rock. No bones were broken but her ankle had swollen considerably and any technical climbing for Caitlin was now out of the question.

"We'll have to go down now." Mark announced.

"I have to go down." Caitlin insisted.

"Oh right!" Mark countered sarcastically. "You'll just stroll back to the campground by yourself and wait for us in the Winnebago."

"I'll take her down." Meadows said. "I'm not really in the mood for climbing. Besides, the two of you could go a lot faster by yourselves. We'll be fine. We'll see you at Rearguard in twenty-four hours."

Both Shimm and Mark wanted to make this climb. They had tried three times before, each time the weather forcing them to retreat before making the summit. It was getting old.

Halfway up Kain face, the weather was quickly changing. Mark was leading the pitch as the icy clouds came up from beneath them. The temperature, which had been in the thirties Fahrenheit most of the day, had quickly dropped into the teens.

It was already dark when Shimm found a small ledge to setup a bivouac. They were now nearly seven-thousand feet above sea level and three-thousand from the ice field below. Shimm set two snow anchors and tied them into the tent. Mark, not feeling confident of the situation, insisted on each man tying in separately with an ice screw so that both would have independent protection.

In the tent with the sun long gone, they struggled to find their respective headlamps. "I don't know what your sister was thinking," Shimm was saying, "It doesn't make sense to come all the way up here and turn around just because you don't feel like climbing anymore."

"She twisted her foot. It was swollen for Chris' sake!" Mark countered. He did have his suspicions about the accident. Could it have been a small price she would be willing to pay for the satisfaction of making his life miserable? "She seemed to live for it, the bitch!" he thought.

He could not believe he was actually thinking that his sister would risk her life just to piss him off, but then again...

Mark understood all too well. At thirty-three, she was still a twelve year old girl that needed to be the center of attention. She claimed to be a strident feminist, yet she also capitalized on every feminine attribute she could muster.

To Mark, stereo-typing women was easy. Mark felt that women were not necessarily weaker, just more prone to enunciate the difficult, play out the pain, in other words — whine.

In Mark's mind, men put up with crap because that's what men do. You don't open your mouth until you're ready to follow it up with some kind of action. Women on the other hand, will open their mouth, begin complaining at the slightest sensation of a gentle breeze. Complain that it's too cold when the temperature went from 72 to 70 degrees. Complain about decaf when the barista gets the order wrong: "Oh! Is this decaf? I thought I ordered regular, oh no worries, this will be fine, it's not what I ordered though, I can live with it, no need to take it back, if it's no trouble thanks, don't want to be a bother. Well, all right if you must, if you're going through all that trouble you could make it a bit hotter next time, thanks."

That's how Mark's mind worked, he focuses on some petty minutia of someone's personality and then he would pick at it like a buzzard. Mark could go ten or twenty minutes without an audience, musing and ruminating about the imperfections in the people around him.

He thought that the real reason his sister turned back was that she had just gotten sick of him complaining about their parents. "People are who they are," she would say.

Their parents had divorced when he was thirteen. Their mother insisted she needed to find herself and instead found an eager spiritual guide willing to do the searching for her. He was a wine salesman who occasionally gave her extra attention at the grocery store where she worked. Together they embarked on *her* journey after a quick but intimate introduction at the local Best Western.

Left to be raised by their half-employed, wholly intoxicated father, the three children created their own family within a family. Simon, his older brother, delivered newspapers on an early morning motor route. Seven days a week, at precisely 2:30 in the morning, he would get out of bed, make a pot of coffee, fill a thermos and proceed out into the weather to warm up his 1973 Dodge pick-up.

Mark was recalling how the truck would wake him every night. No muffler, no money to fix it. For ten minutes, he would let that piece of shit run before he drove it away. He would spend the rest of the early morning delivering papers in that gas guzzling pile of junk. "What an asshole!" Mark mused.

Shimm was fumbling through his pack trying to find a flashlight. "You, know, if we had gone to Half Moon Bay instead of the Canadian Rockies, we wouldn't be here now." Shimm said aloud, ripping the zipper off a small pouch that contained the battery powered headlamp.

"No shit," Mark replied, "and if we hadn't climbed this mountain in the middle of winter we wouldn't be perched on a ledge with a three-thousand foot drop to the ..."

"It isn't winter." Shimm said.

"What?"

It isn't winter. It's fall. You know autumn. Winter doesn't start for eight more weeks. Shimm was satisfied he had gotten the stove to work and was confident in his knowledge of the seasons.

They had known each other since high school. They had grown up in Wenatchee, Washington, spending their free time learning to rock climb in Icicle Canyon and at Peshastin Pinnacles.

The wind was picking up again. The temperature was eight degrees Fahrenheit, according to the thermometer clipped to Marks pack. "It's winter" he insisted.

What pissed Mark off the most about his parents was that after eight years of blessed divorce, they are back together again. His father had quit drinking and had taken up a religious life according to the teachings of some Himalayan guy.

"Now there's an asshole,' Mark thought to himself, not sure in his own mind which man he was referring to.

His mom wasn't doing much better. In fact, she still had the wine-selling-find-yourself guide in tow. Moreover, she wasn't about to give him up. All three ended up living together. Fortunately, we were all grown when that shit happened, Mark thought. "Damn, what assholes!" He found himself saying aloud.

"We need food!" Shimm announced, as he once again began fumbling through his pack. Out came an aluminum container of stove fuel followed by a small single burner stove. Shimm had a suspicion that they didn't have any way to light the stove but he didn't seem to care. The steady cold and lack of food had started to affect him, but neither he nor Mark was aware of the situation.

Shimm found a butane lighter and began a futile frenzy to get it lit.

"You're an asshole!" Mark shouted suddenly. "It's the altitude. It's too damn cold! You'll never light that damn thing. What a moron!" Mark added for good measure, throwing a plastic film canister containing wooden matches at him.

Mark unlocked his belay and stood up on his knees.

"I've got to take a leak."

As he turned to relieve himself out the vestibule of the precariously perched tent, he looked back at Shimm and said, "You know, my whole life has been full of assholes. Sometimes I wish they would all just go away."

As he positioned himself to avoid his own spray in the high wind, his knees slipped beneath him and off the ledge he went. His wish came true.

STALL

Eli Pelican lay in bed trying to adjust his bloodshot eyes to the sunlight slicing though the cheap drapes in his fifth story San Francisco apartment. He had been laying there for over an hour, or so he thought, when he looked again at the clock on his bedside table, it had barely moved. It was 5:55AM

His sheets were wet from sweat. This was April and it wasn't even six A.M. and the heat was sweltering. He still had two hours before he needed to be at work. He brewed coffee and took a shower.

He sat reading the paper, a small story about a powerful black hole near what we would consider to be the center of the galaxy with possibly 'significant' implications for Earth, briefly caught his attention, but he couldn't think about that now. Eli was distracted by the fact his newspaper pages were difficult to separate, as if they were stuck together like Velcro. He seemed to be spending an eternity juggling his thumbs and fingers - he finally gave up. Without warning, he spilled coffee on himself, drenching his shirt and tie. He put his cup down hard, shattering it into a half dozen pieces and dumping its remaining contents all over his newspaper.

Eli looked at the clock. It was 5:58 AM. He had made coffee, taken a shower, read most of the paper and changed his clothes all in the span of three minutes. Something wasn't right.

In the parking garage his car took forever to start. He jingled the ignition, pumped the gas pedal, and finally coaxed the engine to life. The engine sounded rough, his air conditioner was not working, and the steering wheel pulled to the right. He lurched out of the garage into the bright sunlight almost colliding with a milk truck. He noted the time on the dashboard clock it read 5:59. He made a double take - 5:59. He'd been up for at least an hour, but if he were to trust his clocks he'd only been up for six minutes.

Looking down Market Street, he could see several accidents. Traffic seemed slower than usual. Eli turned on the car radio. He scanned his presets but none worked. He finally found a single station, KGO. Sally Reilly was telling her listeners how hot it was, her voice unusually deep and slow.

"Weird," Eli thought.

"It's one hundred and three degrees in the bay area at five fifty-nine, news is next," she droned.

Eli came up to a red light which refused to change. Drivers became impatient. A near collision in the intersection involving two other cars made the road impassable. Like many other drivers, Eli got out of his car and began to walk, no longer sure if he was still on his way to work.

And why was it so hot? Before he could think about that, he heard a loud slow grinding noise behind him. He turned around to look at those two cars that were in the intersection. They somehow collided, when only moments before they had seemed to have stopped.

Henry Glivens set his safety rope and harness just as the sun was coming over the horizon. He had planned on washing all the windows on the east side of the building today, but for some reason things were taking longer than planned. As he peered out over the expansive urban cityscape below him, he observed that the streets seemed to emit a dense cacophony, louder and more disonant than usual. He checked his watch, it was 5:59. He hooked into his Jumar, set his lanyard and took the pressure off of his Prussic descender and stepped off the edge of the building, sliding down to the first set of windows on the sixth floor.

"Is it just me or is everybody screwed up this morning," he thought to himself, adjusting his harness and fitting his squeegee before beginning his first window.

United Airlines Flight 516 was well into its final approach into San Francisco International, when passengers felt a loud and long shudder coming from the right side of the aircraft.

It was 5:58 AM, when copilot Steven Montoya watched the cowling from the right Pratt & Whitney PW2037 engine separate from the aircraft and begin its ominous descent into the city. At the time, he didn't realize it was the result of the failure of the 2nd stage turbine hub blade retaining lugs, the failure of which turned the engine into a busted can of metallic spaghetti. All he and his captain could do is shut down that engine and land with the one good engine, and be thankful there was no fire.

Eli had only walked a single block and again he was sweating. In fact, he felt like he was running a marathon. He looked at his watch again; it was still 5:59! He slowly scanned his surroundings. If he hadn't looked at his watch, he would have guessed the time to be around nine or ten in the morning. Stores were starting to open for business, accountants and lawyers who normally didn't show up on city streets till at least 9 A.M. were already here at six, or 5:59 to be precise.

His thoughts turned back to his energy level, he could barely walk! Everyone around him was slowing down as well; a contagious fatigue.

The engine cowling seemed to fall lazily through the air. The thing about this particular piece of aerial debris is that by the time it would hit the same rooftop that Henry Glivens was hanging from, it will only be descending at 24 miles per hour. What was stranger still, is that it had slowed down instead of increasing in speed. Twenty-four miles an hour was still sufficient velocity to create the force needed to severe both Mr. Given's haul line and his safety rope, which in fact it did, sending Henry Givens on his way to the sidewalk. As luck would have it, Eli Pelican would be there to meet him.

As Henry hurtled toward the sidewalk, he felt pretty sure he would die that day. He was wrong. Time stopped, before Henry did.

GLEASON SNICKEL
(AND THE SEARCH FOR LOVE)

My dad didn't have a clue. He was on his cell phone sending a text message to his brother when he crossed the median and hit an oncoming UPS truck. I was twelve. My dad was dead. I didn't cry. I never really knew my dad. If he wasn't on his computer, he was on his cell phone, his smart phone; text messages, phone calls, web surfing, email. He was a busy guy, until he was dead.

My mom was next to suffer misfortune at the hands of preoccupation. She left our dog Mason in the car while she went to get groceries. She met a friend while shopping and they chatted a few minutes; an hour and seven minutes to be exact. When she got back to the car, Mason was dead, it was August. It was the afternoon. It was California. It was one hundred and seven degrees. Mom was unaware that it would be hot in the car with the windows closed, after all, it had an air freshener.

Pretty soon I'll be by myself. I never thought a kid could worry so much about his gene pool. Last Friday, mom was walking across Main Street on her way to pick up the mail when she received an expected text message. She replied immediately, using two thumbs to tap some seemingly important micro-tome. She neglected to look up when the curb arrived, which she then tripped over. Her forehead made the acquaintance of a steel light pole that was firmly planted twenty seven inches in front of her. I got the mail that day. Mom got nine stitches. Yep, pretty soon I'll be by myself.

I hate Facebook. Mom is on Facebook. My dad wasn't on Facebook; he was into Second Life. He probably wished he had a second life when he saw that UPS truck coming.

These days, Mom doesn't say much to me anymore, especially since dad died. She didn't say much to either of us when he was alive come to think of it. Maybe it was because we weren't on Facebook. My mom thinks we should all be required to get a Facebook account when we get our birth certificate. Her new boyfriend agrees with her. I think he's her boyfriend, even though they haven't met yet. He's still poking her on Facebook.

I'm thinking I might take matters into my own hands. I should run away and join the circus, though I'm not really sure what that would entail; not actually having ever seen one. Maybe that just makes the adventure more... adventurous. I will simply leave.

Lazarus lives next door. He is, in fact, a fat strawberry-colored cat that is blind in one eye. He also happens to have hair rollers melted permanently into his fur. That's because the nine year old girl who put the hair curlers in his hair and then proceeded to blow-dry the already very dry cat for twenty six minutes had been left unattended, by parents who work... for Facebook.

I had my day-pack, a can of warm Coke and the thirty seven dollars that I had saved from two years' worth of birthdays and Christmases. My mom always gives me money. I think she keeps expecting me to buy an iPad or at the very least, a smart phone.

I left the house determined to start a new life. Lazarus and the nine-year-old girl were in front of their house. Lazarus had gotten one of his melted curlers stuck between the boards of their off-white picket fence. The girl was also stuck because she had a leash, one end on Lazarus and the other connected to a harness wrapped round her shoulders and waist, the kind of harness some parents used to keep their cute little tots from running off in crowded malls. I suspected nine-year-old girls' mom had the harness for dangling the kid off of a bridge. Nine-year-old girl was too old to need the harness for shopping mall containment.

Her name was Jenny. Her parents were at work. She said her parents work all the time. Since today was Sunday and there was no car in the driveway, I had no reason to doubt her.

I unhooked the leash and removed the harness from her tiny frame. Jenny untangled the cat from the picket fence.

"See ya," I said, as I turned to leave.

"Where ya going?" Jenny asked.

"Outta here!" I replied.

"Can I come?"

"I'm not coming back," I said firmly.

"Good. Please let me come with you?" she whimpered, trying to put on that 'poor me' face that some girls do so well.

"You got money?" I shot back.

"Six dollars…but I can get more," she replied.

"Go get it, and get some clothes too. Like I said, I'm not coming back."

Jenny went in the house and up to her room, from her bureau she pulled out her favorite pair of Disney Alex Russo jeans and her long sleeve hooded sweatshirt. She also grabbed her favorite book, *Second Helpings* by Jessica Darling. Next, she went straight into her parents' bedroom and took three twenty-dollar bills from a Bible her mom kept in the top right hand drawer of her mom's desk. She put this, a can of Pringles, a Twix bar and a banana into her school pack and headed out the door.

I wasn't sure where we were going, but I knew it was time to go. If Jenny wanted to come with me, who was I to stop her? She was only nine, but I was only twelve!

We walked a block and waited for the St John's 320 bus to take us downtown. It wasn't till we arrived at the bus stop that I realized that Lazarus the cat and his assortment of dangling hair curlers had followed us.

He had a slight limp, no doubt from injuries he sustained while covertly trying to get in the family car whenever Jenny's family was going somewhere. Lazarus wouldn't leave Jenny's side. Not so much because he was fond of Jenny, but because he lived in perpetual fear of Jenny's dad, who would throw Lazarus out of the car window whenever they drove away.

We couldn't take the cat. That was not possible, on buses, trains? How could we feed the thing? We've got less than a hundred dollars between us and no prospects… or plans.

I looked at the pathetic feline, with the plastic melted curlers, the glazed over right eye, and crooked tail. I was inclined to like this cat. I didn't see a cell phone anywhere near him and I was pretty sure he wasn't on Facebook. Lazarus appeared as grumpy as I felt.

"Let's go home," I said, as I picked up the cat and began walking.

"What!" Jenny shouted. "Why go back? Nobody cares if we go! Nobody wants us!"

"The cat does." I replied.

IN THE WOODS WHERE THE WIDOW SINGS

Emma had been walking her dog Angel late Wednesday afternoon as she always did. Her usual route took her through Glover's Park, where over one-hundred and fifty years ago, Samuel Glover had assembled a small stone building to house his cider press.

On this late October day, as for the last ninety years, the cider mill was quiet. A person could detect the scent of decaying apples among the fallen leaves which had accumulated several inches in the neglected park. Emma kicked the leaves wildly as Angel stuck his nose here and there deep into the souring vegetation. Striking a still pose for a few seconds, Angel would suddenly exhale with a large 'woof' and scan the area as if his mysterious prey was mocking her from afar.

Emma was twelve years old. She had lived in Glover all of her life. She had been walking the dog every day after school for nearly three years. She couldn't remember the last time she walked here with her father, but she was pretty sure it was a long time ago. Emma wasn't really mad at him for being absent so often, but she did miss their walks in the park. She remembered the day he brought Angel home. It was the day she had gotten straight 'A's on her report card. Her father had secreted the golden retriever into the house using the back door and he left the dog in her room. It was a good day, she recalled.

Today she and Angel had kicked leaves along the trail for nearly a quarter of a mile. She could see the iron fence that separated the park from the old town cemetery. She was about to turn around when she stopped suddenly. As Angel began to growl, Emma gestured with her index finger to her lips and spoke to Angel in a firm voice, "Shhhhh!" she said. Angel stopped, perking her ears, listening.

Angel heard it first, her nose pointing towards the cemetery. Then, filtering out the soft rustling of the trees, Emma could hear a woman's voice, singing.

Now it was almost dark, but her curiosity was getting the best of her, Emma and Angel slowly moved towards the cemetery, and the singing woman. Emma was careful not to be seen, and stood back in the forest several feet from the fence that separated Glover's park from the ancient town graveyard. She scanned the multitude of old tombstones and memorials while thick clouds darkened the landscape. For the first time, Emma felt uneasy.

Then she saw her. The woman was wearing a white wool jacket and a white skirt, hemmed at the knees. The woman struggled to keep her balance as her high heels sank in the thick autumn mud, a large black hat draped with black lace covered her entire head. She clutched a small white purse.

The woman kept singing, it was a sad song. It was a depressing song. Emma had not heard it before and the words were indiscernible, more like humming, she thought. Emma concluded that the woman did not know the words to the song she was singing, but Emma was satisfied that she was very familiar with their meaning.

Emma wondered whether she would be discovered if the lady looked up. The woman finally did raise her head, but Emma was sufficiently hidden by the darkness of the forest, that the woman never noticed her.

Ashley Middleford never dreamed that her life would turn out like this. She was forty-eight years old. She no longer had children, or a husband. She's was singing the same melancholy tune her mother sang on those late, lonely winter nights, waiting for her father to come home. She kept singing, with no idea what the title of the song was, or for that matter, the words. Somehow it fit the moment. She was staring at a tombstone. She didn't know who it belonged to; 'Peter Burtakowski,' it read, "1914-1998," a long-enough life, she thought.

Her own husband had not been found. She had loved him. Richard had married her and adopted her daughter. Then, one day, he had simply vanished- just like her daughter. She had searched the house, the yard, every nook and cranny she could think of. She remembered calling the police, describing him in every detail she could think of, and some she could not. She remembered how they found his car in the river -- the picture of Al Jardin's tow truck pulling it from the river was plastered across the front page of the Norwich Bulletin, water pouring out of the car's broken windows. Robert was not inside.

Coming to this cemetery every day for months now, Ashley struggled to ease her pain. She had to go somewhere; somewhere gloomy because that was how she felt. It was her daughter Hannah who had first gone missing. Two days, then a week. Had she run away? She was only eleven years old! She would be sixteen next month had she lived. Mr. Gridiron found her decaying body in the swamp on route 169 near Pomfret almost three years ago. He was spraying pesticide on roadside weeds when he noticed beyond the guardrail, a pink scarf in the swampy water at the base of the embankment,.

Her family and her life was wrecked. Not by divorce or disease, not because of some silly argument where they could someday call and make up, but instead by some evil person or group, violent and frightening, by any standards. Ashley often looked into her future and saw no happiness, not now, not ever. Her world had been destroyed.

Emma recognized the woman now. It was Mrs. Middleford. Everyone knew who she was; the funny lady, the not-quite-right in the head lady. Her husband had run off after their daughter was found dead. The police could never prove her husband had killed Hannah, and she couldn't bring herself to think that he could do such a thing. She preferred to think of him as dead. She just went crazy every one said.

Darkness began to settle on the town of Glover. Emma knew she had to head home soon if she wanted to find her way back. She heard a branch crack behind her. She turned to see Angel turning in a circle like dogs do when they want to lay down. Angel did just that. "Angel!" Emma gave out in a sigh of relief.

Sergeant Noel Crispin also knew about Ashley Middleford. He was the responding officer when she first reported her daughter missing. She had been understandably frantic. He remembered calling for paramedics, and she ended up spending the night in the hospital. The second time a missing person's call came from that home, it was for her husband. Again she was delirious with anguish. This time Sergeant Crispin was able to calm her down and even waited with her until relatives arrived.

It was a cop's job to be skeptical. Was Ashley Middleford too freaked out? Was her husband Richard too nice, too cooperative? Was he some kind of pervert? Was she? Over time, everything and everyone had been meticulously ruled out, only the mystery remained.

Sergeant Crispin had wanted to stay on the case, after all, his own daughter Emma was about Hannah's age. He hardly spent time with her. His job, and especially these kinds of cases, took much of his time. Besides, there was one thought that kept haunting him; if it wasn't the father, then it could be anybody, and that meant all of the local girls were at risk.

Ashley became aware of the approaching darkness and prepared to leave. From the woods, she heard a single dog growl, and then a short whimper. She strained to focus, a full moon now offering some added light. That's when she saw the pair of eyes locked on hers, piercing out of the woods for only a moment. "Richard?" she gasped.

SWEET TOOTH

I have a sweet tooth. If I didn't have the good fortune to obtain excellent dental insurance, I would in fact still have just the one. I suck sugar like it is oxygen. The fact that Hershey chocolate bars look like pieces of dog poop in the summer doesn't stop me from jamming them into my face all year long. Sugar is a drug and I am addicted.

During my childhood, my own father was the local sugar dealer. He drove a truck loaded with the stuff, day in and day out: *cake confections* as they were called in *those* days. Jelly-filled, crème-filled, chocolate covered concoctions, with or without nuts, coconut or frosting - I inhaled it all. In fact, if a store couldn't sell it by the time the shelf-life expired, my Dad would take home the stuff and we'd have at it. What others could no longer stomach, our family had for dessert.

In one of my earliest memories -- I think I was two or three -- my parents were about to have a rare night out on the town, without their gaggle of children. When I heard the news, I went into a state of panic. It meant I'd be going to bed early, which was of course, unacceptable! This situation required an appropriate response: a tantrum.

I began wailing away at the top of my not-yet fully developed lungs, I grabbed the bars of my crib and shook violently as only a 1050's Gerber baby could. My father stomped in to the room. I became quiet. He became quiet. He approached cautiously, holding in his hand a package of cream-filled cupcakes a.k.a Drake's 'Yankee Doodles.'

"Settle down now," he said, in his firm commanding voice, "and you'll be able to have this tomorrow at lunchtime. He placed the package of cupcakes on my pillow. Then he bellowed, "Do NOT eat these tonight!"

"How cruel could this guy be? I used to think he liked me!" I quickly stopped screaming and began to plot the nights' mission. I knew that my older sister would be in charge while they were out, and chances were good that she might quickly discover any transgressions that I might commit, and that meant a report to my old man in the morning.

The lights went out. A beam of 40-watt 1955 electric light crept through a crack in the door. As I pretended to sleep, my nearly brand-new blue eyes spied the triple package of Drake's Yankee Doodles just above my right ear. *"Do NOT eat these tonight!"* The words came back to haunt me as if somebody was reading my mind. How was I going to get my Drakes Yankee Doodle Cupcakes without getting caught?

I kicked and thrashed in frustration. Thanks to these shenanigans, the Drakes Yankee Doodle Cupcakes slid down the pillow, cruelly coming to rest a mere few inches from my mouth; the gateway to my digestive Disneyland. How was I to withstand this temptation -- perhaps an even greater temptation than that which Linda Labrea would offer me 12 years later?

I could see the cupcakes just off to my right. I could even smell them. Was there a break in the seal? I turned my head just enough to be able to flick the package with my tongue like a shy garter snake - hoping for a mouse. The package slid even closer to my mouth. I heard the door open wider and the light from the TV filled the room. My sister was checking in on me. I became as still as a squirrel just discovered by a Doberman Pinscher. The light dimmed again.

I wanted to eat the cupcakes, but the thought of that stern look of my father and his accompanied warning *Do NOT eat these tonight!* made my body nearly catatonic while my brain schemed furiously. The idea of actually going to sleep while these cupcakes were so close, so intimate, was impossible.

I started playing with the wrapper. I wasn't eating those cupcakes though, instead my adorable little hands started to squeeze the cupcakes. Suddenly, just the smallest opening appeared on the package seam! I had crushed one cupcake and the white cream began to sneak out of a hairline crack - was that an opening? I brought the pack of cupcakes to my mouth and began sucking- so far, the one activity that demonstrated my sole expertise to date. I crushed the other cupcakes and kept squeezing, Squeeze! Squeeze! Squeeze!

Before long the contents of the package became a packet of nearly liquid milk-chocolate goo. Over the next hour or so, I managed to suck out all three cupcakes without opening the package. The little hole in the seam remained miniscule, while my addiction was satisfied. I could honestly say I didn't eat anything that night. Drinking my cupcakes was clearly outside the scope of my father's original directive, therefore I knew that I would be immune from any intended consequences.

This of course, was the first of many miscalculations in my lengthy career as a problem child.

AWKWARD

The uncomfortable mask was strapped to Blimpkin's beet red face. The mechanical wheezing of the respirator sounded like an old Texas oil derrick. Not that Nina had ever seen one, but she did remember seeing movies about Texas and there were lots of oil wells with those clanging, swishing pumps. They looked like robots kneading dough; wheeze, whoosh, wheeze, click.

His resident medical expert and son Luke Levenplatter had always told Blimpkins he was going to die if he kept smoking. Everyone else in the family had diabetes or something just a bit more straightforward, but he had to go and be different. He just had to go and get emphysema and cancer. Mind you he had been fat, which was strange considering how much exercise the guy did. For a nerdy chemist, he certainly didn't fit the stereotype. Soccer, basketball, kayaking, hiking, even with all of the exercise, he was still overweight, so much so that his childhood moniker Blimpkins seemed appropriate even in later years. His family expected him to have diabetes or heart disease, but somehow the lung thing just took everybody by surprise.

His real name was Robert Peter Levenplatter. He was a chemist for Barren Pharmaceuticals. He had lived nearly 71 years in Natick, Massachusetts on Waverly Avenue. Even though he had been quite athletic most of his life, he waged a constant battle with food. Now, this once chubby gentle ball of human-ness was suffering the final insult. The cancer was quickly sucking the life out of him.

His kids were grown. Faithful daughter Nina taught mathematics at the local high school. Her father thought she could have done better, maybe even have been a scientist considering her knack for understanding organic chemistry. He had shelled out quite a bit for her Wellesley education. And why didn't she ever marry? She was nearly 34 and hadn't shown the slightest interest. It was beyond Robert Levenplatter to consider that she might be gay. Not that he thought it was so bad to be gay or even gay and married, he just never thought about his daughter that much.

Nina's brother Luke had a completely different childhood and a completely different outcome. He was a Trekkie, he was a genius, he had scholarships up the kazoo, and he was accepted to MIT before he completed his second year of high school. He knew about nanotechnology when no one knew about nanotechnology. He developed a carbon dating technique that was identical to the one used for determining the age of the Shroud of Turin as an eighth grade science project. Luke was a nerd.

Now, his father was dying. It was his very own father, not someone else's dad, he was pop, the old man. He'd soon be no more. Luke couldn't help but notice that Blimpkins didn't look as tough as he often pretended to be. Not now. Wheeze whoosh, wheeze, click, wheeze whoosh, wheeze click.

Nina sat in a wooden chair next to Blimpkins' bed. The antique Victorian chair seemed out of place as did the woman in it. Luke was standing with his back to both of them, staring out the window.

Luke searched his brain for fond memories of his dad. They seemed few and far between. His sister certainly had them and so did the nephews and nieces like RPL. RPL would be brokenhearted when Blimpkins finally passes, Luke thought. Although RPL's wife Rachael wouldn't mind seeing him on his merry way. She simply saw Blimpkins as a dirty old man. She had caught him leering at her breasts on more than one occasion, she found it quite unsettling. She had told RPL about it, but he shrugged off the whole idea as ridiculous. He actually didn't do anything, RPL concluded.

RPL was Blimpkins' favorite nephew. No one ever knew why. Blimpkins seemed more comfortable with his nephew than with his own son. And speaking of RPL, the door opened and RPL entered the room giving a hug to Nina with one arm and extending his other to shake Luke's hand.

"We could save him, you know." RPL said.

"What?" Luke looked at him, and then looked away rolling his eyes.

RPL was tall and thin; he'd be an imposing authority figure if it weren't for the fact that he was so skinny. His torso took on the appearance of a pair of wire coat hangers mangled into some sort of artistic expression of plane geometry. He had nearly graduated from Harvard Medical School but was arrested three weeks before graduation for stealing a cadaver from the school's morgue.

"We'd use a pig." RPL replied, "Cadillac has one."

"Cadillac has a pig?"

Yes, and he said we could use it for your dad. How cool is that?"

RPL was smiling as if he had just completed a Rubik's Cube in record time, which in fact he had done on more than one occasion.

"Pigs are pretty much like people, organs are about the same size, a very close genetic code so there is less chance of rejection." He stopped speaking a moment and looked at the floor, rethinking his plan for a fleeting moment, squinting, as if the answer lay next to his left shoe. He suddenly whipped his head up. "Yes, we could do this!" He announced.

"We'd kill him!" Nina shot back, not believing that she was even participating in the conversation.

"Right!" said RPL, "That's why I figure we wait till he's dead. That way we won't get in trouble, and we won't need so many... resources. We just want to make sure he doesn't get embalmed, otherwise we're screwed. Either way, he'd be no worse off than he is now."

The three of them sat in silence, staring at the floor. It was an absolutely crazy idea, but of all the people in the world these three could do it. In the background the steady cacophony of wheeze whoosh, wheeze, click, wheeze, whoosh, wheeze, click, was ever present.

Nina spoke first. "What about his brain, his thoughts, feelings, his soul? How will any of that come back or will it?"

"Neural download." RPL said.

"What?" Nina asked incredulously.

"I admit no one has ever done one on a human, but in theory it should work. It worked on Bosco," RPL replied.

"Your dog?"

"He was hit by a car last summer. I had been thinking about this 'consciousness thing' for some time and I thought it was the perfect opportunity. I did a spectral brain analysis and recorded the data on a flash drive. Seemed to work for Bosco, but I can't really be sure."

"Even if you could do that, how do you do a neural upload to get his consciousness back inside him?"

"I've got an app for that," RPL said straight-faced, unholstering his smartphone.

"Do it," Luke heard someone mutter. All three looked up, it was Blimpkins. Through his oxygen mask, he repeated himself. "Do it," he said.

No one said anything on the way back to the house. RPL was jotting down notes as if this entire outrageous suggestion was a done deal.

"Look, this is absolutely insane. Let's just forget about it now, shall we?" Luke said.

"How can you say that? Your dad has been good to all of us. He helped my mom buy a house. He found a job for me after I screwed up at med school. And he ..."

"He brought me a doll in the middle of the day." She interrupted, memories suddenly flooding her brain. She was only six or seven; she spent a couple of weeks at the neighbor's house while her mom was recuperating from surgery.

"He brought me a doll in the middle of the day." She said again.

"So what?" Luke asked.

"Daddy left work to check on me." Nina continued, "He stopped by at lunchtime to see how I was doing at Liza Macloe's house. Remember we were staying at her house while mom was in the hospital? Leeza had gotten a huge dollhouse and an awesome doll for her birthday. At least I thought it was awesome. I guess I was a little jealous, I was crying. Dad stayed for lunch, thanked Mrs. Macloe and gave me a hug before he drove away. I never felt so alone."

"So what?" Luke repeated the question.

"Daddy came back about an hour later with a doll house for me, it was the same exact doll house that Leeza had, and he brought me an even bigger doll. I'll never forget that." She hadn't called him daddy since she was twelve.

"He never brought me a doll," Luke said. RPL and Nina just looked at him.

It was about 7 P.M. when they pulled in the driveway, Cadillac was already there. He was in the car, dome light on, or so it seemed, an eerie flickering glow played on his face. Actually he was watching videos on a tablet. He had a Coleman stove on the dashboard that he was using to boil water for tea. Cadillac was Cadillac because he never left it. He had a perfectly nice house about two miles away, but he preferred to live in his 1963 Cadillac ambulance which, like so many other ambulances of the day, was a refitted hearse painted white.

When friends said he preferred to live in his Cadillac, that's not exactly true. If he answered honestly, he would probably confess that he would rather be back in his house. The problem was that he couldn't fit through the door of his house. Cadillac weighed four hundred and seventy-three pounds. The last time he was at home he had slipped in the shower, cracking his skull. The paramedics couldn't get him through the door. Firemen had to break the door down so the medics could get him out. He hasn't been back since. That was almost two years ago.

"Is that Cadillac?" RPL asked. "I haven't seen him since his accident.

"Yeah, that's Cadillac," Luke said getting out of the car. "You guys go on in, I'll see what's going on."

With that, Luke, hands in his coat pockets, reluctantly made his way to Cadillac's Cadillac. He opened the passenger door and stood back, allowing some time (and room) for the odors and fast food trash to escape. Then with one arm resting on the roof of the car, he leaned in and took a cigarette from Cadillac who was already igniting his lighter with his other hand.

"What's up?"

"Nothin, Your dad not doing so good."

"Yeah."

"Is he gonna die?"

"Probably."

"That's too bad. He was, I mean he is a cool dude."

"Yeah, he's ok. What did you want?"

"I got a pig for your dad."

Nina Levenplatter did not love her mother. She wanted to, but she just wasn't that loveable. She couldn't imagine her in any scenario that involved affection. Nina thought that her mother was cold, and often wondered if she herself were colder for thinking such a thing. It reminded her of that television episode of Frasier where Niles and Frasier reluctantly go on an ice fishing trip just to manipulate their dad into saying I love you. Unlike the television episode, Nina's mom never did say it. Their relationship had always been on ice. Now, with Blimpkins on life support, Nina had no idea what her mother would do when he passed. Everything about him had been warm. He could warm her, but Nina knew without him her mother would revert to her usual refrigerated self.

Caroline Levenplatter had secrets. Her marriage had been a sham. She had married the wrong man. The one she wanted was dead: dead as soon as their love was born. She had never felt so happy on that one afternoon. She was never to be happy again.

When Luke, RPL and Nina walked through the front door, they found Caroline sitting on the couch staring at the television. It was an old episode of Frasier. She barely acknowledged them and took another long drag from her unfiltered cigarette.

"Hi Mom." Nina said.

"Hey Caroline!" RPL chimed in.

Luke said nothing.

"Your father is dead." She announced to no one in particular.

"Daddy?" Nina shouted, "We just left him!"

"You don't look too broken up about it, mom." Luke said.

"I haven't had time to let it sink in. They just called a few minutes ago." She lied. She had been secretly looking forward to this day for months.

"He's had Chronic Obstructive Pulmonary Disease for three years and fourth stage lung cancer for five months. I would think that would be plenty of time to let it..." Luke wouldn't let her finish the sentence. "Mom!" he interjected.

"Stop it!" Nina ran teary-eyed up to her old room and slammed the door.

Caroline Levenplatter hadn't always been the hateful isolated old bitch everyone thought her to be. Yes, even as a younger woman she might have been a bit cold, a bit standoffish as her mother would say, but she had been very beautiful. That had to count for something, she always assumed, even if it was forty years ago.

She was twenty-two, she was coming around a corner on Brookside Road just south of the country club, when the car hit a patch of ice, and went careening out of control finally ending up over the embankment in a swamp. She wasn't hurt, but her left leg was stuck between the steering wheel and parking brake release. Swamp water was leaking in around the doors and both her feet were soaked. Gravity was forcing the swamp to yield to the weight of the '72 Buick and in a matter of minutes the car would be completely submerged in the black muck. It was Robert Peter Levenplatter, who broke the rear window with a rock, and pulled her to safety. Eventually they began dating and got married as soon as he returned from Viet Nam.

"Luke, go get your sister. We've got to move fast on this." RPL said.

"Are you serious? You can't really be thinking what I think you're thinking." Luke said.

RPL pulled Luke back outside.

"Look, we can really do this but we can't do it without you. You're the only one that understands amalacytase, that enzyme your dad worked on. It seems that it would only be fitting to see if he could benefit from his own discovery."

"You mean use the amalacytase to preserve his cells while you put a pair of pig lungs into him?"

"It would certainly be better than trying therapeutic hypothermia; I just don't see that working for us. I think we should try amalacytase. You're the only one that can do that. I can take care of the transplant and we'll get some help with a surgical suite."

Ever since leaving med school, Luke had been working as a paramedic for Boston EMS, ferrying patients from one facility to another, pulling comatose homeless alcoholics out of trash dumpsters, along with the usual cases of heart attacks and diabetic victims. He knew he could do more.

"All right all right, let's do it! I'll go back inside and get Nina. We'll need to get the body before they send it to the funeral home. We all know what happens in the basement over there. So we'll need Cadillac and his rig for that. If Blimpkins gets embalmed, we're screwed. You can get the pig at Cadillac's house. I'll take Nina and go with Cadillac to reclaim the body. There shouldn't be any problem with two of his children showing up.

Luke went back inside to get Nina. They both knew what embalming really meant. Most people think of it as a simple exchange of fluids and a little dress up; just a little addition of formaldehyde and a nice suit and tie. The reality was much more. Historically funeral directors lived in fear of dead people passing gas at public viewings, making growling noises in their deserted tummies or heaven forbid a bit of ooze running out of the deceased nose or ears at the wake. To make sure there are no unwanted surprises, the honored dead have their blood exchanged for embalming fluid and then have every new and old orifice stitched up in order to block any potential path to embarrassment during funeral services.

Caroline twisted the cigarette butt in her fingers, letting the hot red coal fall into her untouched glass of Johnny Walker Blue. She could hear her husband admonish her about being so wasteful.

"Do you have any idea how much that stuff costs?" he would have said. It drove her crazy, always correcting her, he was right of course, she knew that. He didn't have to remind her. Over the years she realized that she could get at least a little pleasure out of making him equally miserable. She simply began pushing his buttons that pushed her buttons. As long as she thought she was in control, she could live with it; the perfect marriage.

He had been a gentleman when they were young. "He tricked me, that bastard!" she would say over the years more than once. He wasn't really a bastard, but the thought did help to assuage her guilt about her empty relationship.

The house had been quiet while he was away in the hospital: no arguments, no petty bickering, and no sucking his nose mucous everything thirty seconds. The man refused to admit he had allergies, and never even considered blowing his nose. He snorted his nasal excrement right back into those crammed and jammed sinus cavities day in a day out. "It drove me crazy!" She found herself saying out loud.

The door opened and Luke came in sheepishly. "I need to get

Nina," he said.

She's upstairs, go on up if you like."

"Right," he said, stopping on the third step.

"Are you alright, Caroline?" he asked.

"Caroline?" You mean 'Mom' don't you? That's the second time one of you kids has called me by my first name tonight. Yes, I'm alright. It hasn't sunk in yet, that's all." She lit another cigarette as Luke continued up the stairs, but stopped again.

"We'll be going out for a while. Could you do us a favor and clean out the garage? We'll be bringing him back here, you know."

"Bringing him back here?" She asked.

"That's what I was told. Please check on the garage."

Caroline wasn't sure what he meant, not sure if he meant they'd be having the wake and services at home, like their parents and grandparents. Had it been Robert's own request? "Why go check on the garage?" she wondered. She went into the kitchen to get more scotch.

RPL found himself in the dark overgrown back yard of Thomas Cadillac Bernard. There were no lights on in the house, he hadn't bothered to get the key from Cadillac, and he was squinting, trying to adjust to the lack of light. He knew he had to find this pig pretty quickly.

And when he did, what would he do then? Kill it? Keep it alive till he got back to the house? First things first! How was he going to get the pig into his Prius? The only way he could get a 400 pound pig into his car is if the pig got in on its own.

He unlatched the gate, not sure of where he was going. He remembered playing in this very yard with his pal Cadillac years ago, but things had changed. The dog house was gone, the tree house long ago removed. The picnic table, WHACK, was still here. His knee began to throb instantly and he felt faint. Can't pass out, can't pass out, he chanted, until he passed out.

He never thought of himself as a great kisser, but RPL wanted to think he knew at least a little something about kissing. He had French-kissed Rachael Gelling, his one-day-to-be wife, behind the Dairy Freeze back in February of '91. All he remembered was how short she was and that she smelled of Bazooka bubble-gum, which was weird since it was the same gum his dad chewed while he was trying to quit smoking. While kissing Rachael was not exactly the same as kissing his dad, it was still pretty repulsive. He opened his eyes to find a pig forcing its tongue into his mouth.

Nina and Luke were squeezed into the front seat next to Cadillac as he careened down Central Avenue, the smell of moldy French fries, stale ketchup and burger grease filled the air.

"Please don't step on that bag, that's my McRib sandwich!"

"So Luke," Cadillac continued, "We're picking up your dad at the hospital?"

"Check."

On the way back to the house, RPL realized he needed more help. He pulled his cell phone from the clip on his belt and dialed a number. "Raymond, this is RPL, are you busy…right now. I have a favor."

Raymond Lusconi had been a bio-med technician for nearly thirty years. He worked at some of the finest hospitals in the country, most of which were in Boston. He watched not only employees come and go over the years, but also the equipment, the technology; IV lines, inflow meters, defibrillators, sternum saws, gas monitors, infusion pumps, the list goes on. Everything in medicine seems to change but Raymond saw that it always remained the same: stop leaks, keep airways open and deliver fluids. He once wanted to be a doctor, but that door never opened.

That's why he hung out with RPL. Twenty-five years younger than Raymond, RPL was one of the few Harvard students that seem to actually have respect for staff. He was shocked when RPL invited him out for a beer one night. Turns out he did have an ulterior motive. He needed someone with access to the school's morgue and OR suites. In exchange, RPL had agreed to let Raymond stay and watch him practice surgical procedures. Though he had long dismissed the idea of being a physician, he still had a natural curiosity about medicine, biology and anything that he could attach the word 'cool' to. So when he finally got the chance to watch a human being cut open, intestines spread out on a table, he couldn't pass it up. He just needed to be fortified with a solid fifth of Jack Daniels before he did. The night RPL was thrown out of school; Raymond was too drunk to remember.

There was a whole week that he couldn't remember back then. They said he had amnesia, a highway maintenance worker had found him wondering along the road in his underwear. He responded to the name Raymond, and they gave him the name Lusconi after the worker who discovered him. His psychiatric assessment found him to be extremely bright with an exceptional talent for all things medical, so the state funded his technical training, which is when he first met RPL. After the cadaver incident at Harvard, Ray was let go and eventually found work at Brigham and Women's Hospital. He wasn't surprised when he got RPL's call.

"Ray, do you think you can get hold of a gurney, surgical tools, hell, I need an entire OR suite for two patients including anesthesia pumps, IV kits and monitors, paddles - the whole works. Ray I need it now; right now. My uncle has passed away, and we're going to bring him back. Are you in?"

Silence.

"Are you in?" RPL asked again.

"Yeah, where do you want me to bring it?" He heard himself reply.

"My uncle's house, we'll do the operation in the garage. His wife Caroline is there right now prepping the space."

"Caroline, Caroline." There was that name again. Whenever he heard that name, his forehead skewed in a seemingly stalled twitch that took several seconds to dissolve. The name was so familiar, he knew it had significance but wasn't sure how.

When Nina walked into the hospital room, it took everything she had to keep from breaking down. She quickly recovered, absorbing the image of her dead father, lying lifeless on the bed, his jaw dropped, mouth agape and eyes open, staring blankly at the ceiling. She had secretly imagined this day many times. She often wondered why people act so surprised when a loved one passes, and yet she knew, even from early childhood, that we all pass at some point.

"The longer we hang on, the more likely the next day would be the last." She said to herself. There was no doubt that Nina carried the family philosophical gene.

"Not quite the same as being useful, like medicine," her father would say, "but a few people will still appreciate you."

"Badda Bing!" She thought to herself.

Luke interrupted her thoughts as he made considerable noise coming through the door with a gurney. "Grab the sheet from your side of the bed and we'll just move him onto the gurney in one motion. We need to move quickly." He said.

"He's too heavy, I can't do it." Nina said without even trying.

"He's not that heavy, come on, we're running out of time."

She surprised herself as she lifted the body with little trouble, "He's so light," she said.

"Of course he is, he's been sick for years, it's been a long time since he was 250 pounds."

"A long time since he was Blimpkins," she added.

Caroline flipped the light switch in their double garage. Within a few seconds a barrage of neon spread across the room and the space was filled with almost unbearable white light. It was unusually clean as garages go. The walls were lined with work benches, tidy trays arranged in precise order. In fact this garage reflected Blimpkins life perfectly. Each of the four walls represented a different interest, a different expertise, and Blimpkins was expert at all of them.

On the sports wall, an array of kayaks, climbing ropes, cross country skis, backpacks and balls; basket balls, footballs, baseballs, bowling balls and tennis balls. On the wood wall, a cacophony of carpentry paraphernalia, saws, sanders, shims, drills, carving tools, wood planes and wood putty. But that wall was the last wall of a normal garage.

Unlike other garages, where fishing tackle or lawn care products, might be hiding, waiting for next spring, Blimpkins had a chem wall lined with flasks of foaming fluids, vials of viscous venoms, jars of powders with unpronounceable names. He was a chemist by trade after all.

The other wall was the bio wall. Actually, this wasn't really a wall at all, but simply the back of the garage door. Blimpkins had affixed rows of shelving, each growing some sort of spliced and diced cross pollinated genetic concoction of his own making. Everything from fly catching dandelions to red pepper grass, to silanotruvelium avrantis, a plant whose preservative properties might one day have a place in healthcare. It was the source of Blimpkins' proudest achievement, amalacytase.

Luke had told her to clean up the garage. It looked pretty clean to Caroline. She didn't think a car had ever been inside. Blimpkins had spent most of his waking hours here.

Caroline didn't hear RPL's Prius pull into the driveway, so she was a bit startled when she saw the fly catching dandelions, red pepper grass, and the silanotruvelium avrantis start their journey to the ceiling as the bio wall returned to its original functionality and became a garage door once again.

RPL was standing there, waiting impatiently for the door to open; next to him attached to the end of a leash was Petunia, the soon-to-be history-making pig.

"You'll need to sign this release," the nurse said to Nina as she handed her a clipboard.

"Fine, here you go," Nina replied, signing the form and handing it back. The nurse left without another word.

When Nina turned her attention back to Luke, he had already pulled the white dressing gown back to reveal her father's emaciated torso.

"Ok, here's how this is going down," he said, taking a large syringe from the inside breast pocket of his corduroy sports coat. "As soon as I inject this serum, you need to begin CPR and don't stop till we get to Cadillac."

"Inject a serum! CPR! Luke, Daddy's dead!"

"Nina, calm down. This serum is amalacytase. Dad invented the stuff. It will preserve his cells while we work on him. Now you'll need to do CPR to make sure the stuff gets sent out to his entire body. No need for mouth to mouth, not yet anyway."

With that, Luke forcefully plunged the needle into the dead man's chest and kept pressure on the plunger until it was completely empty.

"Go ahead start chest compressions. Hard! " Luke directed.

Nina placed one hand atop the other three fingers above the end of the sternum as she was taught in First Aid class. She began pushing on the chest wall.

"Not hard enough. Nina, climb on top of him and really bare down. We need to move the serum. I'll push the gurney out to the parking lot while you take care of CPR.

Nina, using a step stool, climbed onto the gurney. Hiking her skirt, she straddled her father in such a way to maximize the chest compressions she was about to resume.

"This is weird," she said, realizing the bawdy appearance this position suggested. She began compressions.

Luke forced the gurney through successive groups of double doors, down one hallway to the next, slam, another set of doors, slam, then another.

"You know, I've always suspected you had a special relationship with dad." Luke said grinning, "I just didn't know just how special!"

"Wipe that shitty grin off your face, you little incestual necrophiliatical bastard!" She shot back.

They crashed through the final set of doors and into the late autumn night. The air was filled with the scent of decaying autumn leaves and the smell of coming snow.

A pair of headlights came on in the parking lot and Cadillac pulled up to the curb to meet them. Luke swung open the rear door and the strong stench of pickle, onion and barbeque sauce smacked him in the face.

"Are we going to be able to make a pit stop on the way back?" Cadillac asked, "I'll need to pick up a couple more McRib sandwiches."

RPL was pacing back and forth outside of the garage when Raymond backed the large ambulance up to the garage. As Raymond exited out the rear door he found himself face to face with Petunia and RPL.

"That's a pig isn't it?" Ray asked, knowing full well what the answer would be.

"Did you get everything?" RPL asked.

"I think so." It was kind of tricky getting it all out of there without being seen."

"You stole it?" You stole a half million dollars' worth of medical equipment?" RPL looked Raymond straight in the eye with as serious a look as he could muster. Then they both broke out laughing.

"Hopefully we'll have most of it back before dawn." RPL added.

Together they carried the equipment into the garage and began the work of plugging in monitors, setting up operating tables, sterilizing instruments.

RPL felt that someone was watching him. When he turned around, Caroline was at the side door.

"What are you doing, Robert?" she asked, truly puzzled.

At that moment RPL realized that no one had filled Caroline in on the 'grand plan.'

"...and who is this with ..." She stopped short as her eyes met the smiling eyes of Raymond Lusconi.

"I've heard so much about you. Caroline isn't it?" Raymond walked over extending his hand.

"Yes, Caroline Levenplatter, and you are?"

"Raymond Lusconi, a friend of RPL, It's certainly a pleasure to meet you, Caroline."

Caroline was taken off guard, this man looked a lot like ...but it couldn't be, could it?

What she had never told anyone, was the night she had veered off the road and found herself in the swamp, she had met a doctor a few hours before at the country club earlier in the day. A man named Raymond. They talked for hours, eventually holding hands under the table, eventually wanting much more. It was more than a chemical bonding. It could have been love at first site. That night of the crash, she hadn't been alone. She and Raymond found themselves intoxicated from both the alcohol and the unanticipated carnal gratification. They were driving fast down Central Avenue, then the crash, then the cover-up, then the shame. It wasn't until a few weeks later that she became close to Robert, and he mentioned his missing brother, that she had made the connection. "So Raymond, have you always lived in the Boston area?"

"As far as I can remember ma'am, unfortunately I can't remember all the way back."

"What do you mean Raymond," she asked innocently.

Just then a horn sounded in the street. That was Ray's cue to move the EMS unit so Cadillac could back in with Blimpkins body.

"Excuse me, ma'am," Raymond said as he backed away to the truck.

RPL put the operating tables in place and set up the anesthesia cart while Nina set up the surgical trays, cath-lines and monitors.

Cadillac backed the hearse to the edge of the garage and shut off his motor. For the first time, the driver's side door opened and Cadillac stepped into the open air.

"Cadillac! Are you going to melt or something?" Luke quipped, as they all watched Cadillac waddle to the rear of his ambulatic home on wheels, surprised by the sudden reminder that he could walk at all.

"Looks like you're going to need my help, so now was as good a time as any to stretch my legs," he said adding, "besides; I don't often have the chance to make use of an actual doorway, even if it is a garage door."

Raymond finished setting up the OR lighting and checked the defibrillator. He felt a peculiar feeling in the pit of his stomach, but he let it pass.

"Raymond, you and I will harvest the pig lungs from Petunia over here, I've prepped an area on this side workbench. Bring a bucket with you."

We live in a hi-tech world, a world of amazing discoveries and technological miracles, RPL thought to himself, but to get at the lungs of this pig, I'm just going to quickly slit her throat and bleed her out.

"Luke, can you prep your dad for surgery please, Nina can assist, won't you Nina?"

"Are we really going through with it guys? It's still not too late; we could just let him go, couldn't we?" Nina stared blankly at the corpse in front of her.

"What's going on here?" Caroline interrupted. What on earth are you up to, Luke?"

For the first time that night, Caroline was wide awake. The vision in front of her was surreal; her children and their friends in surgical gowns, a sedated pig lying on the workbench where a skill saw and router had been parked, her dead husband lying on an operating table in the center of the garage, as lifeless as one could be, and there seemed to be no mistake, they were about to perform an operation, on Blimpkins, poor dead Blimpkins!

"Mom, we're going to bring dad back. RPL thinks he can do it. I'm sorry we didn't tell you, it was the spur of the moment, and I just assumed RPL had mentioned it." Luke said sheepishly.

"Bring him back? Bring him back? You can't bring him back. No one's ever come back!"

A flood of memories came back about the night of the car crash; there was somebody in that car with her when it sank. Somebody she loved but she didn't say a word when she was rescued by Robert Levenplatter. She just let his unconscious body sink into the muck of the swamp. She couldn't bring him back, and if she had a choice she would have rather they left her there in the black mud. She hated her life. It had all been a lie. When she refocused she saw Raymond Luscano staring at her.

"It's all right Caroline, if anyone can do this RPL and Luke can." Raymond said solemnly. She wasn't the only one who was having a flood of memories.

"Caroline? Are you my Caroline?" Raymond asked as the full weight of the moment fell on him. It was his Caroline, the love of his life, now an aged woman, still recognizable by those beautiful blue eyes. They had the one afternoon together. Where had she been all of these years?

He turned to look at the lifeless face on the operating table. His confused expression of joy, pain and horror was seen by everyone in the room.

"Is this my brother? Is this Robert?" His words slurring as he brought his right hand to his head and collapsed to the floor.

Caroline got to him first, kneeling beside him, "Raymond, it is me, Caroline!" she assured him with tears in her eyes.

He was still conscious, but was in the throes of a classic major stroke. Luke rushed over with an oxygen bottle and mask. "Let's get him some oxygen and one milligram of epinephrine," Luke said.

RPL and Nina just looked at each other, confused.

"Raymond?" Luke finally blurted, turning to see Caroline's tearing eyes.

"We had dated before I met your father." Caroline said as she tried to concoct some semblance of a plausible explanation. "We were in love until…"

RPL came over and began his examination of Raymond. Nina grabbed the crash cart and the epinephrine, and moved closer.

Raymond was looking at Caroline trying to say her name, now fully aware of whom she was and the life before his accident. She had left him in the car that night. She had left him to die. After the fight for his life in the swamps of a cold Massachusetts evening and Raymond Levenplatter managed to get out of the swamp on his own, no longer knowing who he was or where he'd been.

Caroline turned to Luke, tears in her eyes, and he could see the shame and longing welling up inside of her, all of these years of deceit. He looked down at Ray Luscano, or Raymond Levenplatter and saw for the first time, the familiar Levenplatter face. Over the wheezing and gasping of air, the oxygen mask muffling his voice,

Raymond Levenplatter uttered his final words.

"Luke, I am your father."

He closed his eyes, his labored breathing stopped; the stroke had been too intense to overcome.

"Look in his wallet! RPL commanded, get his driver's license out."

Everyone looked at RPL as if he were insane.

"See if he's an organ donor. We'll use his lungs instead of the pig. If he really is Blimpkins's brother, the odds of this... this ... operation will get considerably better."

They could have argued over the dignity of dead, they could have abandoned the whole idea. That didn't happen. RPL got his wish, they all suspended belief and grief long enough to do what they had to do. Even Caroline, clearly in shock, adjusted lighting as RPL and Luke performed the transplant.

When the exchange of organs was complete, the next problem was flushing out the amalacytase with an acid citrate dextrose solution before adding whole blood.

Nina set up the IV lines while RPL grabbed the correct serum bags and began the infusion. Luke monitored the chest cavity for leaks, so far so good.

RPL was about to close up, when there was a voice from the darkness.

"Don't do it," the voice commanded.

"Don't do it," the voice repeated, this time louder and with even more conviction.

RPL stopped working, put down his surgical instruments and walked over to the garage door. He peered into the darkness as if to challenge the interloper.

Rachael? He meekly offered.

A tall thin red-headed woman, wearing what she thought was a leather jacket with fox fur adorning the cuffs and collar, appeared in the doorway. RPL had given the jacket to her for their tenth anniversary last summer. She always wanted a leather jacket, but he couldn't support the idea on moral grounds, so he bought her a synthetic one and lied.

"If you sew him up before you get that heart going you'll have killed him twice."

"Massage." RPL responded, embarrassed by his obvious oversight.

"Massage." The woman confirmed.

She was right; using a defibrillator on a dead heart isn't going to do anything. RPL needed to stimulate the heart by hand.

"My lovely MacArthur Fellowship winning wife is correct. I'll squeeze some blood into your dear father, while... Luke, have the paddles ready. We'll probably need to stabilize his heart rhythm once we get it going." RPL said.

"If you get it going!" Rachael said. Not waiting for response, she turned slightly to acknowledging the others in the room, and walked over to the wash basin and scrubbed in.

"Luke, start the epinephrine bolus and follow it with a drip and have the paddles ready." RPL said.

Luke nodded that he was set up and ready to proceed. RPL directed him to begin.

Blimpkins opened his eyes but couldn't see anything. He wondered if he was dead. Did the boys actually do it? He wondered? He felt alive, his chest hurt. He could hear the blood pressure monitor's rhythmic 'beep.' After a while the total blackness gradually lifted, and he could make out the outlines of the surrounding room. It looked familiar. It was his bedroom at home. He wasn't in a hospital; he wasn't lying on a cold slab in a morgue. He was alive, again!

He turned his head just enough to see the glow of a computer, he strained his eyes even more before the time stamp in the lower left corner of the screen came into focus. It was 3:34 in the morning. His BP was 109 over 60 and his pulse was 63 -- that much, he could make out. He looked across to the other side of the room, and saw his wife Caroline sleeping in the rocking chair. "She's probably not too thrilled," he thought to himself. He closed his eyes, tried as best he could to ignore the pain in his chest, and went to sleep.

After setting up Blimpkins's bedroom as an intensive care unit, RPL and Cadillac collected the surgical equipment and poor Raymond Luscano's desecrated body. They delivered Ray's body to Evergreen Memorial along with Robert's death certificate. Then they headed back to Brigham and Women's Hospital and returned the OR equipment before the day shift arrived.

Luke and Rachael monitored Blimpkins for the first two hours after he was back in his old room, while Nina and Caroline finished cleaning up.

No one had noticed the surgical equipment had gone missing for nearly 12 hours. Everything was as good as it could be and a dead man is now alive and one that only an hour ago lived is now dead: in some perverse way it was an even trade.

It was early afternoon when Blimpkins woke up again. His wife was looking at him, half smiling, half crying. She was wearing a thin silk blouse that barely covered her bra; he used to call it her over-the-shoulder-boulder-holder.

Due to the unusual circumstances surrounding his operation, Blimpkins was spared much of the routine surgical prep and recovery discomfort. Other than the pain from the actual incisions and stitching, there was no intubation required, so no waking up with that panicky feeling of a tube shoved down your throat. Nor was there the intense discomfort of getting it yanked out. Only the quiet pressure and numbness of a catheter reamed into his bladder and the PIC line that RPL had tapped into his shoulder reminded him that he was alive.

"You'll be as good as new in a few days, Dad," Luke announced as he entered the room, carrying a large tray overloaded with foods, fluids and flowers.

It was a shock to see his father alive, the pink skin, the rosacea around his nose and under his eyes, red, blood flowing, living!

"How are you feeling?" Luke asked.

"I'm doing OK, I guess, I'll sure be glad to get this damn IV pulled out." He said, nodding towards the taped plastic hose in his upper chest.

Caroline took the tray from Luke and brought it over to Blimpkins bedside. "I've got some nice vegetable broth, Robert, and a cup of hot tea, that's all the Doc says you can have for now.

"I want a burger, a cheese burger with bacon and onions!" He shot back.

"I'm glad to hear you say that, dad," Luke replied, "but that's just going to have to wait another day so we have time to flush out any unforeseen problems and make sure we've got all of your systems working."

Luke adjusted the saline flow meter, smiled at his mom and left the room. Blimpkins and Caroline were alone for the first time in months.

"How are you feeling really?" she asked.

"I'm fine, considering," he replied.

"...considering you shouldn't be here at all!" She shouted.

She had heard that cliché all her life in the real world, in the movies, on TV. "You're lucky to be here, Robert. For most people, that meant you're lucky someone saw you drowning and called the medics, or you're lucky you had your seat belt on when the car rolled into the ditch."

"That's what I was considering," he tried to say with a smile breaking onto his face. He stopped talking and looked at her. "What ditch?" he asked.

Tears welled up in her eyes, and she avoided looking at him for a few moments, looking around the room trying to think of something to say.

"Caroline, we both know how you've been feeling for a long time now. The last thing I want to do is put some bizarre, needy type pressure on you to stay together, the clock is ticking on good living time, you know."

Robert," she began, finally looking him straight in the eyes, "there are a couple of things you don't know."

"OK, let's have it. I've got only six months to live?"

"I don't know how long you have to live, Robert, but however long it is, you can thank your brother."

"My brother? I don't have a brother!" He was clearly confused. "Do you mean Raymond?"

She nodded.

"But he's been dead for years." He looked toward her for an explanation, and it finally came.

Awkward.

THE FIRST RIDE

When winter comes to America, kids start thinking about Christmas. Mainly they think about Santa Claus. The snows start in mid-December. Many cities and towns dress up their streets and boulevards with Christmas decorations and colorful lights.

This usually happens on the Friday or Saturday after Thanksgiving- the same day that Santa drives through town on a fire truck throwing lollipops and bubble gum at all of the excited children.

We kids always wondered if there really was a Santa Claus. Ray Snoolley, who was a couple of months older than me, thought it was all malarkey.

"Santa Claus is a bunch of malarkey," Ray would say at the bus stop on the last day of school before Christmas vacation.

In any given year, an unofficial survey seemed to indicate that fewer and fewer kids believed in Santa Claus. The fact that some of those fire truck Santas had obviously phony beards didn't exactly help convince us older kids.

If it weren't for my grandfather Maxim (they called him 'Little Max' in those days), I might have been a non-believer as well. You see, little Max had met the real Santa Claus when he was a boy. Not only did he meet him, but he rode in Santa's sleigh, seated right beside him! I know this sounds farfetched, but it's true.

My great-grandfather, Max Sr., kept a diary about life on his farm in Hopeville, Connecticut during the particularly harsh winter New England winter of 1873.

The original village of Hopeville doesn't exist anymore. Just a few of the original homes remain though new homes have since been built covering over much of its unique history. In the 1870s, it was a thriving community of several thousand busy inhabitants. Most of it, unfortunately, has vanished over time. The original mill is gone. The little school house is long gone, the shops, the market, all gone, Hopeville having been annexed by the town of Griswold many years ago.

The Pepin farm, where Max Sr. raised all of the Pepin children, is now part of Hopeville State Park. The main farm house and outbuildings were torn down in the 1970's and the old dirt driveway coming off of Edmund road is nearly overgrown. But you can still park your car near the iron gate and wander through trails and trees of the old 'Pepin Place', which had been the temporary home of a Mr. Claus and his peculiar family.

So from this point, let me turn the story over to my great-grandfather, Max Pepin, after all, he was there. – GPB

December 11, 1873

Our new hired hand arrived today. My oldest son Max took the wagon into town to fetch him. Apparently he brought his wife as well. Her name is Anna. So now we have Nicolas and Anna Claus living in the old house by the wood shed. Rose, my beloved wife, has taken a liking to them right away. I, on the other hand, am a bit more skeptical. This Nicolas Claus seems to be a little too fat to be much good for farm work, but for the moment I'll reserve judgment.

December 12, 1873

This Anna Claus has made a favorable impression. I do confess that she indeed makes fried eggs better than my wife. However, this Nicolas doesn't seem to be able to keep his mind on his work. Still, I have to admit he works hard when he does work, even in cold weather.

Today it was cold! So cold in fact, that the cows' milk froze in the bucket while I was walking back to the house. At dawn I found Mr. Claus feeding my perfectly good grain to some wild elk that had been gnawing at the fencepost in the south pasture - must have been seven or eight of them. I know it must have been cold for them too, but that was my grain he was feeding them!

December 13, 1873

It snowed today. A good eighteen inches! At dinner, Anna had three surprises for me. Stuffed chicken! I think it was ol' Roslyn tonight, stuffed with my Rose's special nut stuffing. Then Max and Theo went outside with a pail looking for clean snow to make maple candy. It was a great evening until I received my third surprise.

I knew something was up. Anna had made maple snow candy and stuffed chicken. There were pleasant smiles everywhere I looked... then it came.

"Mr. Pepin," Anna put forth meekly.

I confirmed her presence with a slight nod as I packed the tobacco in my pipe.

"Mr. Pepin, you are a generous man, and my husband and I wish to thank you so much for your kindness in offering my Nicolas employment at your wonderful farm."

"Oh brother," I thought," they're going to ask me for a year of wages in advance. I know it."

"Mr. Pepin, you have worked very hard and it doesn't seem fair to have made ..."

"Get to the point!" I blurted, not realizing the gravity of this discussion.

Anna continued, "My sister Corinth Kringle has died, Mr. Pepin. Her husband passed away long ago, leaving five children with no place to go."

So that was it! Now I not only have to keep my own family alive, but someone else's as well!

"And where did your sister live?" I asked, stalling for time to think over this new development.

"She lived in Austro-Hungary, sir."

"I see, and you expect me to take these young Kringles in, do you? If they are from Hungary, why not have them stay with some relative there?"

She paused for a moment, almost in tears. My wife Rose came into the room to comfort her.

"Don't be such a mule, Max!" my wife barked at me.

"I just wanted to know why anyone would send five children across two continents and an ocean just to sleep in a crowded little shack on my farm?" I replied.

Anna looked up at Rose, who nodded her encouragement and said, "They don't have to come, sir, they're already here."

That was my third surprise. These children had been hiding in Claus' house the whole past week! They were peculiar too. That's why they didn't stay in Hungary. They didn't grow like the rest of us. They stayed small. Dwarfs or 'little people,' Claus had said. No one would have them. All five were teenagers and not one was more than three feet tall!

Naturally to avoid the wrath of God and more so the wrath of my wife, I agreed that they could stay through the winter, but then some other arrangement would have to be made. After all, I had a farm to run.

Even now as I write this, I see through the window, Mr. Claus in the pasture with those elk, feeding them my grain again! He tells me they are not elk, but reindeer. He's no longer making any effort to hide those 'little people.' My Lord! They're all standing out in the pasture at eleven-thirty at night feeding and petting wild elk! God help us.

December 17, 1873

It's starting to feel like Christmas around here. Max and Theo have been busily making a cutting board as a gift for their mother.

Rose and Anna have been stockpiling meat pies and fruit cakes to take to the Strander household later this week. The Stranders lived a couple of miles away on an isolated farm.

Old Joe Strander has taken ill with the consumption. Misfortune seems to follow the man everywhere. Two of his sons were killed back during the Civil war, leaving only one grandson Donald and his three year old sister Pearl, their mother did not survive her second childbirth.

I've noticed that Nicolas has been doing his work quite well, even though occasionally displays odd behavior. He has purchased an old sleigh for himself and his new family. He spends almost every evening mending and cleaning it. Still I don't know where he will get a horse for it.

Maybe I should consider this at Christmas. He tells me that he has an honest plan to obtain some means with which to pull it, but I don't see how at the salary I am able to provide.

December 18, 1873

I awoke at three in the morning to the sound of chickens squawking. Someone or something had gotten into the barn. I put on my housecoat and boots, took a candle in one hand and grabbed my rifle with the other. The squawking continued as I ran across the drive toward the coop. I hesitated for a moment and thought I might get Nicolas to assist me. I looked toward his house and was surprised to find a light in the window. Then I smelled coffee and... bacon! He was having breakfast in the middle of the night! Just as I turned to continue my search for the trespasser, I was knocked to the ground by some small blunt object.

Sitting there in the snow, I could make out a small person in front of me! "Who's that?" I demanded, "Who's there?" I said again, raising my gun in the general direction of the shadow.

"Don't shoot! Sir, it is only me, Ella Kringle, Nicolas' niece, sir."

"What's that in your hand? Come now, out with it!" I was delighted to have caught someone in my chicken coop after all these years, even if it was just a young child getting into mischief.

"What's that in your hand, child? Give it to me! Give it here!"

Without waiting for a reply, I quickly thrust out my hand and blindly grabbed at the contents of hers. I immediately felt the warm gooey contents of several fresh eggs ooze out from between my fingers, then drip quietly onto my gun.

"I tried to explain, sir, they are eggs for my uncle's breakfast. I am very sorry to wake you, sir." I got up from the ground brushed off the snow, at the same time I unknowingly applied a thick coat of egg white to my pajamas and cap.

"Go to my house and get five eggs from the bowl and say nothing of this, child."

"Yes, sir, thank you, sir!"

I made believe I was inspecting the chicken coop until she returned to her house with the eggs. Once she was inside, I quietly approached the lighted window of Claus' house. There they were, all awake: Anna, frying bacon while Nicolas polished an elaborate silver harness of some kind. All the children were up as well, carving and painting... toys!

December 21, 1873

This morning at breakfast I told Rose what I had seen the night before. It appears as if this family never sleeps!

"Max, look here!" she began, growing more impatient by the minute, "These poor folk have come all the way from Finland to start..."

"Finland! Anna told me they had come from Hungary, off the boat not eight weeks ago."

We both stopped short. For the first time since their arrival, Rose began to get suspicious as well. We peered out the kitchen window at the Claus home. Nicolas was outside feeding my grain to those elk again!

"He looks awfully ridiculous in his red pajamas out there in the snow," quipped Rose.

December 23, 1873

It began snowing in earnest today. More than two feet of snow on the ground and it continues to come down. If the wind picks up some of the smaller homes in the area could be completely buried by drifts. Little Max took some pies and cakes to the Stranders today. He's going to stay overnight and return in the morning. I should have sent Claus with him. He is only sixteen years old and the storm seems to be getting worse.

I haven't seen much of Claus lately. He either works in the barn or he works in his home. Though I admit he takes good care of the animals. And those little people! I've never seen a quieter collection of young people in my whole life. Rose has made them all sweaters for Christmas, a formidable task to be sure. I suppose I could give Claus the old mare, Lizzie for his sleigh. We'll see.

December 24, 1873

It continued to snow today. At the noon meal, Claus, Anna, Rose and I ate quietly. Everyone was thinking of little Max who had gone to the Stranders the day before.

"He'll be alright." Anna said, knowing what was on everyone's mind.

Rose looked at me and asked "Maybe you and Nicolas could go after him today to make sure he gets back safely. It is Christmas Eve, you know!"

I would have liked to, I wanted to tell her, but Max had our only sleigh, and there was no way a horse and buggy would make it through this weather.

"Max?" Claus broke in. "Max, we could use my sleigh, the one I've been working on..."

I appreciated the thought, but our old mare could not survive this kind of weather, especially up Bishops Crossing road, and I told him so.

"Thank you, Nicolas, and you Anna, but I'm afraid little Max will have to take care of himself. He'll be alright."

"I'm sure he will," Claus added.

This afternoon, Claus and I kept busy shoveling snow off the roofs of the barn and houses. The weight of snow had been known to collapse more than one man's home. As I was putting the ladder up to the side of the house, I heard a faint yell for help coming from the direction of the road. I shouted to Claus and made my way up the driveway through the deep snow, finally getting to the road. White bearded Claus surprised me by being at my side when I arrived.

"It's little Donny Strander," I said. "Get him to the house quickly."

After several minutes of warming and a cup of hot cider, the boy began to speak.

"You must come to my house quickly, Mr. Pepin."

"What's the matter, son?" I asked, not trying to sound too

alarmed.

"Where is Little Max?" Rose asked, her patience running out.

"He has been hurt ma'am," the boy said, shuddering as he spoke, "He brought us pies yesterday and spent the night keeping the fire going. This morning he went outside to get fire wood and the whole wood pile collapsed on top of him, it was weighted with so much snow. I tried to dig him out but I couldn't." The boy began to cry.

"That's not all, sir. The house is filling up with smoke. All of the windows and doors are covered with snow. I think the chimney is blocked; my whole family may be suffocating, sir."

"Nonsense!" Claus burst in. "We will simply go fetch them and bring them here."

He seemed to particularly relish the excitement and took command of the situation. I felt compelled to let him.

"Max," he continued, "Get several blankets and some food. Rose, make this boy comfortable. We'll have this lad's family here in no time!"

He looked deep into his wife's eyes and said, "Anna, we've got to start sometime. Get Ella and the others. Max, meet me at the drive in ten minutes." Claus hurried out the back door.

Anna turned to the young boy and said, "Nicolas is a special man. He and Mr. Pepin will make everything right, you will see!"

I fetched the food and blankets and proceeded outside into the snow blown driveway. It had stopped snowing and the sky was clearing rapidly. As the sun set, the air became quite cold. This Christmas Eve wasn't turning out exactly as I planned. "How are we going to get to the Stranders without a horse?" I thought to myself. Surely Claus means well, but I hate to say it, he must be a little short changed in the old noggin.

Just then, the five little Kringle people came scurrying from the Claus home, all carrying burlap sacks. I could hear Claus mumbling in the barn to someone, apparently struggling with the sleigh. I got to the barn and opened the door just in time to see Claus drive his sleigh out into the drive, being pulled by the wild elk he had been feeding. I was dumbfounded.

"Those are elk!" I reminded him.

"They are reindeer, my friend! Now, are you coming or not?" Claus demanded to know.

I stood there for a moment looking at the shiny silver harness, the one he had been secretly working on in the middle of the night. The sleigh had been polished and painted; red seats, gold rails, white and blue trim, all so intricate. I had to admit it was beautiful.

"Do you think it's a mite gaudy?" Claus asked with a wry smile.

"Let's go fetch your son, eh, Mr. Pepin?" With that I jumped in, the Kringle children piling sacks of blankets and food in behind me.

There was no –clippity clop– when deer pulled a sleigh. We just flew down Edmond road through the covered bridge at Hopeville Pond, past the little school house at Hopeville Four Comers and on up the steep hill of Bishop Crossing Road.

The wind was freezing my mustache as we sped past Polinski farm and down another steep hill.

"Careful here," I cautioned Nicolas, "it's a sharp turn and steep to boot!"

"Fine," was his reply.

He actually looked as if he was having fun. We slid down the steep grade and made the sharp turn to the right faster than my fastest horse at an all-out gallop. These elk seem to be just the thing for snow travel.

We were on Roode Road now, whipping past the Tyler home. It was dark and we couldn't make out any house. We went right past where I thought Strander's house was. I strained my eyes to see through the night. I looked again. The Strander home was completely covered with snow. I motioned to Claus to turn the sleigh around, which he did with amazing agility.

I started shouting, "Joseph! Pearl! Max!" No replies were heard.

Claus said, "We've got to get in somehow. If we don't, they'll suffocate, if they haven't already."

"Max is under the woodpile, I've got to find him." I said.

Claus pointed to the roof. It too, was covered with snow, but I could see the chimney exposed a few inches.

"Max," Claus said, "find an axe. Find an axe quickly!" Claus said again. Both Claus and I went around the house wading through the heavy snow, moving and probing towards the place the woodpile would be. It seemed hopeless.

Just then I felt my foot hit upon something... the chopping block... it... the axe!

"I've found it, Claus!" I shouted at the top of my lungs even though the wind had finally died down.

"Give it here. You keep looking for little Max."

I didn't need to argue. I started digging through the snow with my hands... with my feet.

I kept shouting. "Max! Max!" I kept hoping.

Meanwhile, Claus had mounted his sleigh and was calling each reindeer by name. He brought the sleigh and reindeer up the snow drift and perched the sled right on the roof of the house. He grabbed his axe and began beating at the chimney, breaking it apart making the hole larger and larger, until he could fit himself through, which he did, and landed in the living room below with a loud crash.

Each moment came more quickly than the last, but still no sign of little Max. I turned up every stick of wood, I overturned every log. I kicked at every inch of snow. Something pulled at my pant leg. It was Max! I brushed away the snow. He was only half conscious.

"Father", he muttered and then passed out.

I carried him to the front of the house. I shouted for Claus. He had opened the front door and was digging through the drift.

"I'm here Max, dig over here!" he kept repeating. I followed his voice and soon our arms met in a snow tunnel.

"Both the father and the girl had fainted," Claus said, "but they should be alright once they get warmed up." Looking me in the eye he asked, "How is little Max?"

I told him the situation. The boy felt very cold. It seemed that if he were going to live, he would need a doctor immediately.

"Max," Claus said, "warm up the girl and her father, wrap them in blankets and use the Strander sleigh to bring them to your home. I'll give you my lead reindeer Rudy to get you back safely. Since these deer of mine like to move, I will take little Max to the doctor now."

It made as much sense as anything I could come up with, so I agreed. Claus was already lifting little Max into his arms when I turned to fetch the others. Once inside, I immediately remembered the food and blankets I had left in the sleigh. When I went back out, there was no sign of Claus or Max. The Stranders' sleigh was ready and waiting. With a single reindeer harnessed to it. On the doorstep, he had left the blankets and food, and a little toy doll for Pearl.

It was about midnight when I finally got home. The little Kringle people were all up with Rose and Anna waiting by the window. They all came rushing out to assist me with Mr. Strander and young Pearl, who were now both conscious but very tired.

I was trying to think of some way to break the news to Rose about little Max: about how he may not make it: about the seemingly magical heroics of Nicolas Claus. I didn't want to mention the awful cold though, about how I found him buried alive in the dark cold woodpile. We walked into the kitchen. I began to speak.

"Anna, I must tell..."

"Quiet! You old mule! It's about time you got home! Now come say hello to your brave son, Max."

I looked into the fire-lit drawing room to see little Max and Claus sitting in rocking chairs, sipping hot cider.

"Max! Max! How did you? How could you?"

Claus gazed quietly towards the fire. Little Max came over to me and put his arms around me.

"Thank you for finding me, father." he said.

I couldn't believe he was here. Six hours ago he was near death in the out of doors.

"Son, how did you get here? I mean... so fast?"

"Claus, father. His sleigh actually flew through the air. It wasn't a cold ride either, Father. It was warm. I could look down and see all over Connecticut on Christmas Eve."

The boy had suffered a terrible trauma, so I wasn't about to dispute his claim of sleigh flight. Claus' sleigh was fast, but fly? I don't think so. I went over to Claus.

"I don't know how you did it, but I want to thank you for saving my son and the lives of our friends. I don't have much here, but you and your family are welcome to stay as long as you wish."

Claus got up out of the rocking chair and took my hand. "Mr. Pepin," he said, "It is you who needs to be thanked. You have taken in my wife and me, but also my unexpected children."

"You have helped your neighbor in time of need, and have provided the world with an admirable example of child-rearing in your young son Max, who risked his life to help his friends. It is you, and people like you we all must thank.

"As for your generous offer of employment, I'm afraid I will have to decline. I have grown accustomed to these reindeer of mine, and I'm also quite comfortable driving them through the snow, so with your permission, I will take my leave of your generosity and find my own domicile in a more northerly climate, where I may discover a fulltime use for my little hobby."

Turning to little Max, Claus said, "To you I leave the memory of our little ride, Max. Let's say it was the first ride, the first of many."

The next morning we found in our living room, a large beautifully decorated Christmas tree. We had been so busy this year, none of us had even thought of putting one up. Underneath it lay many beautiful hand-carved presents, as well as fruits, cakes and pies. Claus, his wife Anna, and all five of the Kringle children, along with the sleigh and elk... I mean reindeer, were gone.

ABOUT THE AUTHOR

Bryant's world is a battleground of between the likes of Hitchcock and Twain, between fantasy and fable, a compromise of satire and science, of time travel and tall tale, but mostly just good fun.

Gary Paul Bryant writes blogs and story stories, articles and RFPs. He's also an award winning songwriter and composer. He resides on the shores of the great Pacific Northwest with his pet barnacle, Ryan.

***

Did you enjoy reading The Phone, and Other Short Stories? If so, I would greatly appreciate your taking the time to write a short review at Amazon. If you want to know when my next release is coming out, be sure to sign up to be notified at http://www.garypaulbryant.com